PRAISE FOR *THE YEARNING*

'Mashigo is a gifted storyteller and does so with ease and sophistication, bringing a remarkable tale to life in a way that is completely new and uniquely hers, but also familiar to anyone who believes in the existence of invisible powers. *The Yearning* is a herculean feat, not just because Mashigo is a first-time author, but because it is a damn good book that any author will have wished to have written.' – *Sowetan*

'What starts as a tale of love and friendship about a young woman in Cape Town turns into something far more complex and unexpected. There are flashbacks to a childhood in Soweto, slices of a harrowing and life-changing incident, a swirl of sangoma ritual and a touch of family conflict. The result is compelling and heady.' Bridget McNulty, *Sunday Times*

"Mashigo's talent is otherworldly. Marubini is beautiful, sexy, frightening and vulnerable. Simphiwe, like his sister, is a cocktail of love, grace and freakiness. The grandparents stole my heart. There were times I was so scared for a character, I had to leave the book and go do something completely unrelated. This writer knows how to write love in its messiness, illumination, wonder, deliciousness of all kinds. Her treatment of the erotic and unpacking and orgasm is breathtaking. This novel is a highly spiritual, evocative, transformative project. It's about intergenerational knowing, ancestral memory, African women created universes of self-love. It's not about easy or predictable ways out of any hardship." – Pumla Dineo Gqola

THE YEARNING

THE YEARNING

by Mohale Mashigo

With 'From Sweet Valley High *to* The Yearning' *added for this edition*

PICADOR AFRICA

First published in 2016
This paperback edition published in 2017 by Picador Africa
an imprint of Pan Macmillan South Africa
Private Bag X19, Northlands
Johannesburg, 2116
www.panmacmillan.co.za

ISBN 9781770105522
eISBN 9781770105539

Design and typesetting by Fire and Lion
Cover Design by K4
Front cover photograph by Aila Images (via Shutterstock)

Printed and bound by

FROM *SWEET VALLEY HIGH*
TO *THE YEARNING*

My friend Vuyo wrote one chapter and then I would write the next one; that's how we started writing *Sweet Valley High* fan fiction (of course, we didn't know there was a name for it back then). We were just obsessed with reading the books and writing our own stories. We had not planned to write Elizabeth and Jessica as racially ambiguous teenage girls who belonged in California (Sweet Valley) but were somehow living in our world – Soweto and Yeoville in Johannesburg. Girls like us didn't belong in books, so we ripped the ones from our books and pasted them, through the magic of fan fiction, in our pages. Every now and then our favourite singers would show up as love interests, much to the delight of our teenage readers, who were our classmates.

Many years before I co-wrote racy fan fiction with Vuyo, I was reading *Pippi Longstocking*, Roald Dahl's books and many others written for children. The school library was a sanctuary when other children became tiresome. Distant lands and children on adventures occupied my days and nights.

The distance between me and the children in the books became very apparent when I read my first 'grown-up book' – *The Colour*

Purple by Alice Walker. How this book ended up in my possession, is one of those details blurred by memory and time. *The Colour Purple*, to my complete surprise, was a book about black people. The only stories about black people I had encountered were panel storyboards (made up of photos) in the back of *Bona/Pace* magazine. The speech bubbles above the photos of young nurses were my guide as I taught myself to read.

I didn't know I was looking until I found myself between those letters. Do any of us know we're looking till we see ourselves – right there in the pages? All our complicated feelings, barely touched history and quirks coming alive in words. There in the pages I saw myself in The Colour Purple, *sitting alongside Celie watching the drama unfold. Laughing when Mister is finally left by himself and crying when Celie and Shug finally reunited.*

Perhaps Vuyo and I were painfully folding ourselves to fit into the books we loved so much. Nobody was writing about our childhoods in apartheid South Africa or about how confusing it was suddenly to discover that you're a sexual being and have no guidance (just urges and questions). The world of black teenagers in South Africa was missing from the literature we had. Yes, later in high school, it would be Tsitsi Dangarembga who would unfold some of the literary corners I had reduced myself into. Ms Simleit (my high school English teacher) introduced our class to *Nervous Conditions*. There they were: people I could be related to (my uncle was Zimbabwean). These people occupied the entire novel and it was about them; the minor details were included too. These young African women were spread out through the pages, revealing their beauty and shadows.

Their families were so much like the ones I was linked to through neighbourhood or blood. *Sweet Valley High* fan fiction died when Tambu entered my life.

It was *Ways of Dying* by Zakes Mda that really pushed me to find my voice, as a writer and a person. The way in which Mda told the 'painful ugly' effortlessly with compassion and humour, encouraged me to write without fear. I wrote my novel for myself, to be quite honest. It was both therapeutic and entertaining to write these flawed women without interruption or judgement. It never occurred to me that the story I was writing wouldn't be mine forever. Once *The Yearning* was published, however, it ceased to be mine. As a first-time author, I had no idea what to expect. My favourite revelation is that readers will stop me in the street or while I'm minding my business to say 'Hey, wena Mohale, we need a sequel. I have so many questions!' That is one of my favourite things about meeting fellow readers; the passion.

Stories matter and so do the voices of storytellers. When I first started writing *The Yearning* I wondered if anyone would be interested in the life of a woman very much like myself. It is the very same 'doubt' that keeps coming up in questions I get from young writers. Could anyone possibly be interested in the life of a boy/girl like me? It is a question I still get when young writers email me or call me for advice. The answer is never satisfactory – your story matters and so does your voice. Who can blame them for thinking that they do not belong in the literary world? I often feel that way and I am now 'part' of this world.

How do we remedy this? We keep writing, show up for each other, read outside of our comfort zones, give different voices a platform, buy self-published books, read each other's stories and never forget – all stories matter.

The Yearning is my small contribution towards putting us (who are barely in books and stories as whole people) in literature because we do belong. Our stories are valid. It is especially important in a country that has for many years let stories get buried in unmarked graves. *The Yearning* had been rejected so many times that I was convinced it was not a story worth reading. With encouragement from friends, I began to look at self-publishing. Money was saved, strategies were written on a white board in my dining room and final numbers came to 100 – that's the number of copies I could afford to print. Ma was a huge part of my marketing plans, she was going to harass church ladies into buying copies of her favourite (only) daughter's novel. Pa was to stand at the gate and accost young people who would eventually buy the book because they would grow tired of his sales pitch. Looking back I can see that perhaps my marketing strategy was not the best (ha!).

My editor, Elana Bregin, convinced me to try one more publisher. Had I not, Ma would no longer have any church friends. Elana showed me that it is the duty of those on the 'inside' to let outsiders in through the trapdoors. And that while trapdoors may exist, it is better to have the doors open to all.

My aim was to sell 100 copies of this novel, with the hope that somebody somewhere would see themselves in the story. Looks like I've achieved that (and a little more). If a girl from Soweto can go from (racy) Sweet Valley High Fan Fiction to *The Yearning*, imagine the millions of stories that are just waiting to be written and read. Your story matters.

Mohale Mashigo
March 2017

THE YEARNING

My mother died seven times before she gave birth to me. I am grateful for that corpse that somehow always seemed to resurrect itself. My father is gone but his smile is alive on my brother's face. There is no life without death; the two rely on each other and we rely on them both for our purpose. A new mother knows her purpose when she holds her baby within her and in her arms for the first time. A man's work has its purpose in death, as part of his legacy. Why then do we love the one and despise the other? Why do we sacrifice so much of the present to hide the past? Why do we take away the future's knowledge of itself in order to make the past seem perfect? My brother only knows a father when he looks in the mirror. The Yearning haunts him. My mother turns away from the traditions of the past. The Yearning confuses her. I speak as only half of myself. The Yearning hurts me. The life in me came at the cost of another's but I refuse to apologise for that. A part of who I used to be has vanished and I'm now faced with the possibilities of who I could be. The Yearning never stops till we embrace everything that brought us here. In our quiet denial, The Yearning devours us.

THE NAME

M y grandmother often says she regrets giving me my name. 'Children always live up to their names. And you did more than live up to yours.' She shakes her head sadly and laughs as she says this. It is an unbelievably hot day in Soweto and Nkgono is on one of her rare visits to us. She has never been shy to share her dislike for Soweto. 'My child ran away to be here. I don't like this place. I never will.' Nkgono was always laughing, even when saying things that seemed tragic.

'Your mother was having a difficult pregnancy and you took a long time to arrive,' she would tell me. 'Such a stubborn child!'

I loved listening to my Nkgono tell the story of the day I arrived.

'Your father had been driving like a crazy man. Your mother decided at the last minute that she wanted me with her. It was a long way back from Pietersburg and he didn't want to risk missing your birth. I also wasn't comfortable with my only daughter being left alone with that *ngaka* aunt Thoko of your father's at such a time. That's the reason I didn't complain about his driving. Your Ntatemoholo had also wanted to be there, but I didn't want my plants and animals left all by themselves. He was the only person I trusted with my plants.

'Shelling peanuts was the only thing that kept my mind off how fast we were going. Jabu was anxious; new fathers always are. The silence hung between us until we pulled into the dusty yard of the four-roomed house your parents lived in.

'Your mother Makosha was sitting on the stoep, grinding away at a stone with her teeth. My poor daughter – she looked absolutely uncomfortable with a fully baked baby inside of her. We thought for sure you were going to be a boy, because of the way she was so ugly. Thoko was boiling something smelly in the kitchen, so I sat out on the stoep.

'"Ma, I'm scared." That was all your mother said to me. Thoko stopped staring into the brewing smelliness and came over to greet me: "This grandchild of ours wants to stay the entire ten months." Jabulani busied himself with carrying my bags into the second bedroom, while we mocked Kosha about how ugly you were making her.

'The Soweto people were complaining that it was too hot; I live in the heat, grow food in it and have even raised a child under that relentless sun. Thoko said it would rain soon. There was not a cloud in the sky but I believed her. Your mother had just started her garden. The sun was not allowing it to flourish. "There hasn't been rain in weeks. That is rare for Joburg summer," was Makosha's explanation for the state of her sad garden.

'Thoko brought Makosha the smelly brew in a cup and sat down next to me. The three of us just sat there staring at the pathetic garden in silence. Thoko looked at me and said, "I was telling Makosha that Jabulani can help the baby come, but she doesn't believe me." I smiled because Makosha hated talking about sex with me. She knew exactly what my response to Thoko's statement would be. "Oh please, Mam'Thoko don't get my mother started," she said, with red gravel in her mouth. She craved the taste of earth more than anything when she was pregnant with you. I smiled and pulled peanuts out of my pocket. Thoko was saying exactly what I had told your mother. Just before your father came to fetch me I was telling one of my neighbours that sex was what would bring you into this world a lot faster than anything else. Sex brings babies into the world all the time.

"'Ma, the nurses at the clinic told me that I must just walk and that will help."

"'Walk to where? You trust the nurses over me, even when thousands of mothers have trusted me with their daughters?"

"'Hai Maria, you know children never trust their parents," Thoko said, signalling to her daughter-in-law to drink the concoction. Makosha put the cup down and tried to stand up. Her dress was wet.

"'The baby is coming ... Jabu!" Eehhh this child of mine! Sitting with women who are there to help her deliver and she calls out for her husband. Jabu came running out of the house but Thoko waved him away and helped me take your mother into the bedroom. Hooo the scene your mother made! She was crying for her husband, acting like she was the first woman in the world ever to give birth. Thoko grabbed hold of her face and looked her in the eyes. "This is not a man's place. Those pains are going to get worse but you and your baby know exactly what to do, *sisi*." That seemed to calm her some. I was standing by the window in the second bedroom that Thoko had prepared for us to sleep in. "Don't worry, *wena* Thoko, that stubborn child is not coming any time soon. Let Makosha shout until she can't."

'Eventually your mother stopped crying and we told her exactly what was going to happen. Things she had already heard but was suddenly fearful of. What happened next is something nobody can explain. I knew you were ready to emerge, and the room suddenly grew dark. Thoko stood by the window and said it was starting to rain. There is no way of knowing this for sure, but I felt the rain hit the ground the same moment you crowned. The stubborn baby turned out to be a girl. Your mother took one look at you and started crying again. You had finally arrived and you were alive, breathing, screaming, humming and beautiful.

'I always tell people that you just slipped out with no fuss and nonsense. Your mind was made up and you stepped out with nothing but the past behind you. You looked like a queen from an ancient civilisation, so regal and certain. That's why I gave you that name: Marubini. You were a new beginning for us who had lived long lives and needed respite. Marubini is where our past lies, the place of old from where we once came. You emerged and brought us into the future. Thoko loved the name and nobody objected to me giving you that name. Jabu wanted his first child to have only one name and that's why we didn't give you a "school" name too.

'Your father, Marubini ... what an incredible man. Jabu never doubted himself. Once his mind was made up there was no discouraging him. Heh, he is the person who brought my child back to me! Ei, your mother was so troublesome you know? She just left home. Did what all girls who have too much power and not enough sense do: ran away from what she thought was the problem. Then one day she stepped out of your father's car, unsure whether we would welcome her back. Well, you know Peter doesn't know how to stay angry. He was just glad that his only daughter was back home finally.

'Jabulani introduced himself and said he was returning our daughter to us so one day he could ask for her to be his wife. That day you were born, you wouldn't stop crying once you had started. But when your Mama held you, then you stopped. The past was really behind us. Everything changed once you were born. The summer rains fell and Makosha started paying attention to her garden. That same garden that was dry and dying ... The rain that you brought with you revived the garden and your mother's love for gardening.'

I can't say for sure how much of Nkgono's story is true. But I liked hearing it. Every year on my birthday, she still calls to tell me the story of how her daughter gave birth 'to a beautiful but stubborn granddaughter'. We all have the desire to be special. The story of my birth made me feel extraordinary. I was born and I revived my mother's love for gardening. The little garden that was saved by *my* rain became her florist business that kept our family alive. I am blessed to have matriarchs who hold their own even when the ground falls from beneath their feet. But even the sturdiest trees fall if the wind is strong enough. My father's death devastated my mother and the child she was carrying at the time. Her ability to cultivate couldn't save her garden. It seemed like every tear that was shed took life out of the plants and vegetables in our backyard. The soil dried up and nothing grew there again while we lived in that house. Luckily my little brother didn't suffer the same fate as the garden. As soon as Simphiwe was born, I felt like he was mine. That may seem a strange sentiment for a little girl to have, but it was obvious that Ma didn't want to get too close to him, not in the beginning. He came out light yellow-brown like my father, not deep brown like me and Ma. He was too much of something she had lost. So I helped Gogo Thoko look after him while my mother went to work, or lay in bed looking out the window.

Even though she kept him at a cautious distance, I knew Ma loved Simphiwe. Sometimes when she came home from work she would sit down in the kitchen and just hold him; smell his hair and kiss his little fingers. Gogo Thoko would spend the day with Simphiwe while I was away at school. My first years of school were horrible. I cried most mornings because I just wanted to be at home. I was so used to spending week days at home with my Ntatemoholo, my mother's father. While other children were at crèche, I was with my grandfather. Gogo Thoko said that it was okay to cry because I had lost my grandfather and father in such a short space of time. '*Kodwa*, the crying has to stop eventually, Marubini.' I really didn't want to cry. In the evenings I was content to wait for Ma to fetch me at Gogo's house after work. Then we would take a taxi home and Ma would have her time with Simphiwe in the kitchen, kissing his fingers and counting stars on his toes. She would put him on her back and go outside to work at reviving her garden.

The house was very quiet when Ma and Simphiwe were in the garden. The TV would be on but it may as well have been off because I couldn't concentrate. I came to prefer the silence, just sitting and watching Ma outside trying very hard to get her garden back to its previous state. But it was futile. Baba died and so did the garden. All we had was sadness and anxiety. Ma went to bed with it and I woke up in its arms. I would be washing myself in a big metal dish while Simphiwe was getting his morning bath, all the while reminding myself that school was not a bad place and that Ntatemoholo and Baba would not like to know that I was crying for no reason. As soon as the minibus taxi stopped outside my school the panic would set in. Lwambo was the man who drove the minibus that took me and the other kids to school and back. Everyone was used to my tears by now so they just ignored me. I didn't mind because I craved to be left alone. Ma would stand at the door waving until we turned the corner. The further we got from home, the sadder I became. By the time we arrived at the school I would be crying quietly. But the crying didn't remain quiet for long. It became a full-scale meltdown as we were sitting down for the lessons to start. Ma enjoys telling Simphiwe how his sister 'almost became a primary school dropout' because the teachers were tired of my tears.

I don't know why I'm thinking about these old things now. The words in the report I'm supposed to be working on have started blurring. At this point there is no use pretending any useful work will be done. My apartment is quiet, the TV off as usual. Muffled laughter and unfamiliar voices filter through the walls from next door; my neighbours seem to be having a dinner party. Fridays are a break from my usual steamed vegetables and fish dinners. The plan was for Pierre to come over but judging from the lack of communication he is probably working late at the restaurant again. How did a smart girl like me get stuck with a man who *never* has time for anything but work?

I sit alone at the table, thinking back to the day we met. I had just started my job at De Villiers Wines and everything was new.

Not only was I feeling completely inadequate, but my colleagues were constantly questioning my presence. I had only lasted a year in advertising, in a job I had come to hate. That ivory-tower world made me feel far removed from people. The clients were okay, if you didn't mind them throwing their weight around, reminding you that your job wouldn't exist if it wasn't for 'the budget'. It was the people I had to work with that finally made me quit. Most of them thought that taking a two-hour Township Tour that ended at a tourist-friendly drinking spot was a good way to get to know the 'target market'. It didn't help that all too often the 'target market' was me, my family and the people I knew. I grew tired of being accused of 'overreacting' and 'reading too much' into the crappy campaigns. My colleagues had stopped asking for my opinion, even on campaigns that I was involved with. They just couldn't get why I would object to the fact that black people were portrayed dancing; why would they be dancing, when the advert was for tea?

One day during lunch break I just started looking for new jobs. There was no point in staying on in advertising; we weren't meant for each other.

I didn't know anything about wine when I applied for the vacancy in the wine farm's marketing department. De Villiers Wine needed to put some 'colour' into their team, so they hired me. I spent two weeks following the wine from seed to bottle and distribution. Eyes and doubts followed me around the tiny office. All my preconceptions about people stomping grapes to make wine were shattered. Winemaking was actually a very technical and scientific business. I immersed myself in the world of wine. No time to eat or sleep much. I was working for one of the country's oldest and most established wine farms. The pressure was beginning to consume me. It was the worst possible time to organise a birthday dinner for a friend.

'Nobody here yet? Am I early?' The birthday girl, Unathi, stood in the foyer, clutching at the hem of her party dress. Her long legs couldn't keep still, shifting her weight from one foot to the other. As the designated organiser of this celebration, I smiled to show her that everything was going to be just fine. I didn't blame her for sounding anxious. I'd arrived late because Stellenbosch is far away from Cape Town and I'd been locked into a late afternoon meeting that had gone on for far too long. Unathi was already there when I arrived. True to her usual panicky nature, the first thing that came out of her mouth was '*Aphi ama-lady*? Where is everyone?'

Unlike me, my best friend is super-organised. She's the kind of person who doesn't just remember your anniversary but sends you a reminder to get your partner 'that thing he mentioned he wanted that day we met'.

'Unathi, calm down, it's not even 7.00 yet. They'll be here. Some of us work for a living, you know.'

My stay-at-home-mom friend wasn't at all hurt by my outburst. It just rolled right over her. We seated ourselves at the bar of La Cuisine, her favourite restaurant in Mouille Point. She ordered a fruity cocktail for herself and a glass of wine for me. An overly chatty waitress showed us to our table and my head started pounding; there were only four chairs at the tiny table. I had my back to the birthday girl but I knew she was wringing her hands. With my business smile fixed to my face, I explained the situation to Ms Chatty. She didn't seem to understand the enormity of the error. Ms Chatty didn't get the chance to do more than mumble inaudibly before she was cut off by my demand to see the manager 'immediately!'. At this point Unathi was looking around nervously, suspecting, correctly, that I was about to make a scene. She moved closer to me and said, 'Please, Rubi, don't.' I put my overloaded handbag down on the table and counted to ten, something Unathi recommended I should do whenever I felt that I was going to lose my cool.

I was on my seventh recount when a calming male voice greeted us: 'Good evening, ladies, I'm so sorry about the mix-up.' As soon as the voice appeared, things started to happen around us: tables were re-assigned, extra chairs brought up and in moments we were being led to our new, much bigger table.

Unathi was busy putting away the tissue that she had ready in her hand, just in case things went from bad to worse and she couldn't control her tears; that girl is always prepared. I was looking back towards the door where our party had, thankfully, started to arrive when a hand was extended towards me across the table. It belonged to the owner of the calming voice, who turned out to be the owner of the restaurant too.

'Hi, I'm Pierre; please let me know if you need anything else.'

I couldn't quite place the accent. He handed me the handbag that I had left on the previous table.

'Uh, are you wearing contacts?' Unathi asked him in her tactless way, as if it was the most natural thing in the world. This made me take a closer look at him; and there they were, those green, gorgeous eyes, staring out at me from that caramel face. A perfectly chiselled face, the caramel rising at the cheek bones and dipping into beautiful craters that appeared when he smiled.

Unathi kept staring as he shook his head and answered the question he had probably been asked all his life. I couldn't look away from him either; it was as if he had accidentally turned us into statues. Summer possessed my body and it seemed to have forgotten how to move. I could feel the pools of sweat forming inside my silk top. He didn't look like he was trying to keep us there intentionally but there we were, the three of us; us staring at him and him smiling at us. He himself was stuck there too, trying to pull himself away from this process of turning our flesh into fire. Finally his gaze moved from us to the women arriving at the table, and he was able to escape in the distraction.

'That was nice,' Unathi sighed.

Nice indeed! All I could think about for the rest of the night was that delicious mix of caramel skin and gorgeous green eyes.

The intercom goes off; it's the building security downstairs, informing me that I have a visitor. I tell them to let her up, knowing it's Unathi. A few minutes later my best friend is standing in my kitchen, pouring herself a glass of wine. 'Why didn't you invite me over? Woo, it's bad behaviour to drink by yourself, *sisi*.'

I just laugh.

'Serious, Marubini.' She's smiling, though – I can tell from the way she says my name.

Nkgono says she regrets giving me my name. But I don't think my name is the problem. The real problem is all the lies.

THE FATHER

L iving so close to the sea is calming. It's a weird thing to say, for a girl from a city that gets its nickname from how bright and loud it is: 'Gauteng Maboneng' – City of Gold and Lights. I find the sea calming for unconventional reasons. I am so used to having a constant soundtrack: cars, gunshots, people arguing, music from nearby parties, dogs barking and all the other commotion that only a native of Jozi grows immune to. The sea is just another song on the soundtrack to my life. The suburbs would drive me crazy: no noise, no close neighbours, just the occasional dog barking or the sound of patrolling security vehicles making sure the occupants of the quiet houses are safe from criminals ... and noise. Having the sea so close to where I live quiets my mind; it slowly puts me to sleep at night and sees me off when I drive away in the mornings. Those still summer nights, when the sea and the moon look into each other's eyes and whisper to each other like secret lovers, are when I find it hard to sleep. Tonight is one of those nights. My body is restless, constantly tossing and turning in bed. I long for some kind of noise to accompany my breathing.

In the morning my couch has an occupant it didn't have last

night. One long arm is dangling off the edge of the sofa, the other on his crotch. I guess Pierre came to see me after all. I have become used to strolling through from the bedroom to find my boyfriend sleeping on the sofa, shoes on, shirt off, the fridge door half open.

'Pierre, please my love, go to bed,' I say, for my benefit more than his. He doesn't move. I walk over to the fridge and close it, head across to the sliding door to open the curtains.

Unathi strolls into the room and smiles sheepishly: 'Shoo, I could wake up to the sight of your man any day, gal. *Yo, muhle umuntu wakho*, man!'

I accept the compliment on Pierre's behalf and slap his stomach, pleading with him to take his morning snooze to the bedroom. All I get is something slurred in French.

Outside, the day has started without me. The sun is already doing its job and the people of Mouille Point have come to life. The Promenade is abuzz with health freaks, old people needing kisses from the sun, and young married couples who no longer speak to each other, too busy pushing their offspring and checking their pedometers. An elderly couple is jogging by, laughing. Weird! If I was that old I would make sure I slept all day. An old homeless woman tries to stop the couple to ask them for money, food or both but they carry on jogging happily as though they don't even see or smell her.

This *bergie* looks more tired than any *bergie* I've ever seen. Her face has been disfigured by cheap alcohol, the soles of her feet are sticking out of her tattered shoes and she is ranting angrily with two big backpacks on her arms. The nature of Cape Town's homeless, better known as *bergies*, is very endearing in a twisted kind of way. They are generally cheerful people, beg only on occasion and otherwise ask for nothing more than to be left alone. The *bergies* are part of everyone's lives; not in a come-in-and-join-our-braai way, but definitely in a there-is-nothing-more-we-can-do type of way. You know you've lived in Cape Town for a long time if you have at least one witty anecdote about a *bergie*. First-time tourists are often alarmed by this. 'Oh no, this would *never ever* be allowed in Germany,' they lament. 'We don't have homeless people there.' By their third visit back to one of the world's most beautiful cities, they don't even comment on it. *Bergies* are not unlike Table Mountain. The mountain is majestic; it has a life of its own and was here long before us. When I first moved to Cape Town, I couldn't stop marvelling at how it seemed to be watching me, no matter where I was. Now I use it as a way to direct people: 'Are you driving away from or towards the mountain, Unathi?' Perhaps the name 'bergie', 'of the mountain', is a very fitting one.

Watching this *bergie* carrying all her baggage made me think about my own ...

The sound of my phone ringing disturbs my thoughts. I walk over to the table but the ringing stops before I can answer. It's a call from my mother. Pierre wakes up and looks at me reproachfully as if I had planned for my phone to ring loudly at 11.00 a.m. and interrupt his beauty sleep. He stands up slowly and mumbles, 'Hi, I must have fallen asleep while I was thinking about something to eat.'

Unathi smiles at him and says, 'Hi Pierre.'

My honey beams. 'Hello sexy, what are you doing here?'

She shrugs and points accusingly at the three empty wine bottles on the kitchen table. Pierre laughs and shakes his head. 'I'm going to shower, babe.'

Unathi and I have breakfast outside on the balcony and take in the sea air.

'I can't believe you used to live in Joburg. You love Cape Town so much,' Unathi says.

'I love the sea ... but I'm not so sure that it's Cape Town that I love.'

'Do you like it more than Soweto?'

'No, but I feel better when I'm close to the sea. Less anxious, you know?'

'I get that. And my family is here now. This is our home.'

We stare at the sea. I'm thinking that as much as I like Cape Town, Soweto will always be my favourite place, specifically, the house where I spent afternoons with my Ntatemoholo. My father had left us to follow the Calling and my mother's father had come to stay with us. I'm passionate about the sea, but it's so far away from the place that I love the most.

'Well my husband and child are out of town, so can we please do something fun, Rubi?' Unathi says, sipping her tea.

'Fun? *Wena*? Okay what do you want to do?'

She ignores my jibe and says, 'It's a lovely day; let's go have lunch in Camps Bay.'

'Babe, you really don't have to be here. Go to work,' I say to Pierre.

'Why do you always do that?'

'What?'

'Push me away when I choose you over work. Don't you want me here?'

'Pierre, I don't want to fight.'

'Then take this for what it is, okay?'

I knew what I was doing but I didn't know how to stop. Or maybe I'd just given up trying to do damage control on my more destructive behavior. This afternoon's lunch by the beach had turned into a very late lunch and much alcohol was had by both Unathi and I. Pierre was there with us but he only had two glasses of whiskey and kept hinting at needing to go to the restaurant later. Which is why we left before the real Saturday evening 'festivities' started. I wasn't even mad at him for cutting short my time with Unathi. It was only once we got home that I realised it wasn't work he was looking forward to, but quality time with me.

The afternoon was going pretty well until my mother calls again. Mama has a way about her, she knows just how to get under my skin and scratch at the bones. Then she will make me feel bad for letting her get so close to the bone in the first place.

'Hello?'

'Hi, *o kae?*'

'Oh hi Ma, I'm fine. I was actually ...' Before more slow and slurred words have the chance to fall lazily from my mouth, she cuts me off, talking about my cousin getting married soon and questioning me about why I haven't been in contact with the bride to be.

'Mama, I called her when you told me she was getting married, what more must I do?'

'The two of you grew up together. Why *o le so wena mara?*'

'Why am I like what?'

'*Ke* cousin *ya hao. Batho ba tla nahana hore o* funny.' That was my mom, always worried about what people would say. 'People' wasn't another person, 'people' was always her. My mother is people and how dare I upset people or go against their wishes?

'Mama, what must I say to her?' I ask, on the verge of throwing my phone on the floor.

'Just find out how things are going. Why must I always beg you to do something?'

Beg? *Beg*, she says? My mother never begs anyone. She only deals in orders and threats. We go back and forth like this for a while and then she ends the conversation because I am not complying. She has to have the final say as always.

'This is family, *ya hao* and you couldn't care less. When are you gonna come and help *ka di* arrangement? I'm doing the flowers, but it would be nice if you could help.'

'And just leave work?'

'Hooo *o* selfish sometimes, *o a tseba*, Marubini. What about family?'

'What about Simphiwe's school fees? How can I help pay for that expensive boarding school in Maritzburg if I just take off work?'

A moment of silence and then a sigh, 'One day when I'm dead *ke bona batho ba tla ho hlokomela*. Shoo, I raised *ngwana o* selfish, *watseba*. I wonder if *ntate wa hao* could hear you, what would he say?'

Threats about being orphaned and having no family to look after me were always followed by laments of what a selfish child a good woman like her had brought into the world. And always, without fail, the stinging reminder that my father was not around.

She hangs up and I curl up on my sofa, wishing she was dead instead of him.

'Baby, are you listening?' Pierre asks. I nod and rest back against his chest. It's a lie, of course; I haven't heard a word that he said.

Not that it matters, because it was probably something about how I should trust him, which I do. Sometimes I want him there, other times I feel like I'm keeping him from doing things that he loves. I've been feeling this more and more lately, especially now that he's working on opening up a new restaurant. It's crazy, I know, but that's how most of our fights start. I question his intentions and he tries to reassure me, until we find ourselves arguing. I decide that this time I will just lie back against him and enjoy the fact that he is choosing to be with me instead of at work. Here is the man whom I love so much and I'm having one of my moments of madness that could spoil everything.

I kiss him out of guilt; he senses that I'm not doing it for pleasure but he doesn't say anything. 'I'll go to the restaurant later; besides, Natalie has everything under control.' He smiles, and the ice Ma threw on me begins to melt. Perhaps Pierre taking a half day off isn't such a bad thing after all. I get to spend what's left of the afternoon in bed with him.

'What are you smiling about?' I ask, pulling the covers up to conceal my hardening nipples.

'Nothing,' he replies, pulling the covers down again to marvel at my naked body. Why he does that I'll never know. It always causes me a little bit of discomfort, but it also turns me on to know that my bare body elicits that kind of response in him. His eyes travel over my thighs and I feel my immediate response.

I know what's coming next and it excites me. There is a visitor making her way to me, and I can't wait. She packs her bag at my stomach and slowly slides down to where she knows she needs to be. She pulls the rope and the bell in my heart starts ringing, beating faster and faster. The visitor starts unpacking her bags and I smile with anticipation. She knows what she came for and she's not leaving without it. I start to breathe deeply, biting my lip hard and trying to stay in the moment. Closing my eyes I feel Pierre's weight on me and I let him deal with the visitor the way only he knows how to.

'I love you,' he whispers, and makes love to me, giving my visitor a piece of him in exchange for a piece of me. It is here, in this togetherness, where everything is okay, where we tightrope-walk the line between pleasure and pain, clarity and confusion, love and fear. It is here where we should be all the time. This space exists for repairing and escaping and we are doing both. Gently rocking the wounds shut, driving out any doubts with the force of our bodies. We climb and descend. The visitor leaves and I close my eyes, drenched in now.

'Shit!' Pierre is running around in a towel trying to find something to wear in my closet.

'*Ke eng?*' I'm not sure how I managed to sleep through his shower but the commotion of banging doors and drawers has definitely woken me up.

'I'm late. I promised Natalie I would be there at 6.00 and it's already 7.30.' He carries on cursing. Instead of helping him get ready, I lie in bed and admire his body. There is something very beautiful about his skin colour; it's Brown. Not chocolate brown, not burned-brownies brown. Brown. It's Brown with a mind of its own.

Once, when I was ten, I tried to melt a caramel bar. I was fascinated by how a solid bar became liquid. I watched it as it started to bubble. The bubbling caramel put me into a trance; I imagined myself swimming in the warm caramel.

Simphiwe's scream pulled me out of the caramel. I ran into his room to find him sitting there with a stapler in one hand and his index finger in his mouth. Injuries like that were regular occurrences during school holidays. With nothing to do, my little brother would always find something to injure himself with: a splinter from a broom-stick sword or a split lip from sliding in his socks outside on the stoep. I laughed, relieved that he was not crying and that there was very little blood involved. With my usual big-sister charm I took the stapler from him and patched him up with a Mickey Mouse Band-Aid. Off he went to go and find something else to hurt himself with, which turned out to be a stone that got stuck up his nose.

By the time I got back to my caramel pot, it had melted. All that was left of my bar was a stain at the bottom of the pot and a sweet, pungent smell. The burn stain was the same beautiful colour as Pierre's skin, which has the same hypnotic effect on me as the bubbling caramel pot did.

'I have to run. *Au revoir, mon amour,*' is all I hear as he hurries out.

'I like that French shit!' I scream, just as he shuts the door.

'Say "*Dumela* Ntatemoholo", Marubini,' Ma said to me as I was finishing my lunch. Gogo Thoko had made me lunch while Ma went to go and fetch her father from the bus stop. Ma was driving Baba's VW Beetle but she was a really nervous driver. Baba had been teaching her how to drive before he went off to be healed by *amadlozi*. Now there stood Ma's father who was eyeing me strangely. Gogo nudged me and winked, trying to ease my tension. My father had gone off to be with *amadlozi*, something that I barely understood. Before Ma and Ntatemoholo arrived I was interrogating Gogo about my father's whereabouts. 'Why don't *amadlozi* want uBaba to be with me? Why do they live so far away? Why can't I go there?' Gogo just smiled and told me that my father was learning how to heal himself and other people with the help of ancestors.

'Gogo, *ke bo mang madlozi?*' She sat down and pondered for a while. 'Marubini, why are you always asking these very simple questions that I can't answer?'

After a few minutes of silence my grandmother said, '*Amadlozi* are the people who have passed on and look after us. They hold some very important secrets and know more than we do because they are in a different place.'

'And Baba has gone to this place?'

Gogo shook her head. She said Baba was going through something called *ukuthwasa*. It was like school for special people who were able to communicate with and learn from *amadlozi*. According to my grandmother, there was lots of studying through the night and Baba didn't want to disturb us. Still unconvinced, I carried on eating my lunch and watched Gogo move around the kitchen, tidying up.

Once Gogo had left, to go back to her house, it was just the three of us in the house: Ma, her father and me. Ma didn't seem so sad anymore, laughing all the time and speaking in a language I didn't really understand. When I enquired what language they were speaking, Ntatemoholo informed me it was Sepedi. He told me that I was a township child and that I spoke bits and pieces of many languages. The people around me understood me perfectly, so I wasn't too worried about not speaking Sepedi. I enjoyed being a 'township child'.

I kept Ntatemoholo at a safe distance that weekend; observing him from under a chair or while I was pretending to look for weeds in the garden. There was always a smile on his lips and in his eyes, like we were playing a secret game. When Ma left for work I took a vow of silence. This Ntatemoholo and I didn't even speak the same language, and he had made fun of mine already. I insisted that Ma give me a bath before she left and she did it without complaint.

'You know that Ntatemoholo is my father and he loves you very much?' My head nodded, but my mind wasn't quite made up. When we emerged from our bedroom all clean and smelling nice, Ntatemoholo was in the kitchen making soft porridge. Somehow that impressed me. I was the sun's alarm clock. Now it seemed there was someone else in the house who was also an early riser.

When or how my vow of silence ended is a mystery. Ntatemoholo possessed magic that could turn anything into a game. All meals were an adventure and there was always a reason to smile or laugh. Ma was glad that our first day went well, because crèche had not worked out for me. I hated it and cried every morning and hid under a table all day. The food was bad, the other kids were mean and nobody understood me. The teachers had given up on me participating. They knew that I liked to stay under the table and would join my class only when I felt like it. They thought I didn't hear those ugly things they said about me. But I did and I refused to speak to them. Now that Ntatemoholo and I were best friends there was no need for crèche. Baba had thought I was too young to be left at school all day anyway. Ma just shrugged her shoulders and said, 'Well then you have to find a solution, Jabu. Marubini is so stubborn and those crèche ladies are ready to kick her out.'

Baba had stopped working because *amadlozi* were making him sick. The doctors didn't know what was wrong with him. So I stayed home with him for a while. Now that my father was away 'at school with *amadlozi*', Ntatemoholo was the person who stayed home with me.

Ntatemoholo and I started growing morogo in the garden. I had never had wild spinach before. Every morning I would run out to see if our morogo had grown big enough to pick and cook. Ntatemoholo thought this was very amusing. When we took our daily walk around the neighbourhood, he would tell everyone how well my morogo was growing. I loved our afternoon walks. I was never sure where we were going. Sometimes it was to have tea with Ntate Mkhwanazi.

Ntate Mkhwanazi was an old man who lived two streets away from us. Ntatemoholo was very fond of him. We visited him often. He couldn't come and visit us because he was too frail to walk all that way. He always sat outside on his stoep, greeting people who walked past his house. His house was on the way to the shop, so we stopped at his place for tea. I wasn't the only person who was fond of Ntatemoholo. Everyone loved him. He remembered everyone's names, even the mean little girls who didn't want to play with me. On days when I was playing by myself, he would give me a few cents to go and buy myself Cadbury's Chocolate Eclairs and get him some peanuts at the spaza shop next door. Then we would spend all day talking and laughing. Sweet Cadbury Eclairs in my mouth and peanut shells around our feet: those were my favourite days.

Most evenings Ntatemoholo cooked us supper and it was all things that I had never had before. There was sorghum porridge that was sour and mushy in the middle. He would make that with chicken feet. On those days Ma would walk into the house and open the pots. The look on her face told me that she loved having her father live with us.

Ma had started sighing a lot since Baba made the decision to go away and learn how to be a healer. She sighed over the pots while making supper, and in the garden when pulling out weeds. Now that her father was living with us, I noticed that she was smiling from the minute she walked in through the door. Ntatemoholo loved being with us but he also missed his wife, Nkgono, very much.

Nkgono was supposed to be the person who was coming to stay with me, but she couldn't. I heard Ma and Ntatemoholo talking about her important work that she couldn't leave. Ntatemoholo insisted that I call Nkgono 'Koko', which is the correct Sepedi name for 'grandmother'. My memory failed me every time I was supposed to say Koko.

'Come, Marubini, let's go and call *bo*-Koko *ba lena*.'

I never understood why Ntatemoholo insisted on speaking about everyone like there were many of them. Everything was plural: *bo*-Mkhwanazi, *bo*-Ihoko and *bo*-Koko. It would just be one of those things that I didn't understand because I was a township child. When he did call Koko, he would always shout too loudly into the phone. I would sit on the stoep and listen to my grandfather shouting to his wife on the phone. There was laughter between them and updates about their stubborn grandchild Marubini. Koko always wanted to speak to me too. No matter how loudly I spoke, my grandparents would tell me to speak louder. So eventually the phone calls with Koko, Ntatemoholo and me could be heard by all our neighbours.

'Nursery rhyme?' I say, as I sit on my boss's desk. I'm feeling dizzy, but Koos is smiling at me because he thinks I am just winded by the bad idea presented by the advertising agency that was pitching to us. I try to miss as many meetings as I can with the agency folks and have opted instead for a status meeting with our entire in-house team.

'I wish you had been there, Maru. I know you would have told that pansy exactly what you thought of his idea.'

Koos Joubert is the only person who calls me Maru. What started out as a half-assed attempt at pronouncing my name had become a pet name.

When I first arrived at De Villiers Wines, Koos said that he didn't need any help marketing wine. I believe his first question to me was, 'What kind of wine-drinking black are you?' He obviously thought he was being funny.

I knew he was nervous, but I wasn't going to let him think that I was someone to be trifled with. My response was, 'Should I report you to HR for racism now or later?' I could tell that he was both embarrassed and angry.

My smart mouth did nothing for our relationship. I spoke to Unathi on the phone every night complaining about my 'evil colleague'. She'd listen then ask me to look at what I may have done to provoke the 'evil guy'. 'Don't punish him for the sins of those cocaine-head former colleagues of yours, Rubi.'

Unathi was always annoyingly right when it came to these things. Much has changed since my first difficult weeks at De Villiers Wines. Koos and I have become very close; a relationship that goes way beyond the office walls. He has just been filling me in on the advertising agency's idea. De Villers wants to reach the 'emerging' wine market and the agency has suggested using the tune of a well-known nursery rhyme with a few hip-hop 'rhymes' overlaid on it. Trust a Cape Town agency to come up with a crappy idea like that one. I put it down to a lack of contact with black people, not a lack of creativity.

The 'crappy idea' can't be to blame for my sudden dizzy spell, though. Maybe it's because I skipped breakfast.

I'd been against the idea of hiring an outside agency in the first place and Koos knew it. But he'd insisted that we at least let them pitch and give them feedback. Now he looked like he regretted it. 'This nursery rhyme nonsense won't work for us, Maru, that's obvious. I wish I'd never gone along with this whole pitching thing in the first place.'

To change the subject I start singing some of the nursery rhymes from my childhood. Koos joins in with a few of his own. Some of them I don't know but others I vaguely remember from primary school.

'*Bobbejaan klim die berg, so haastig en so lastig. Bobbejaan klim die berg, so haastig en so lastig ...*'

'*Haasie, hoekom is jou stert so kort? Haasie, hoekom is jou stert so kort? ...*'

'I can't believe you know these songs, Maru!'

'I was taught Afrikaans from Grade 2, Koos. For a long time I called Little Red Riding Hood "*Rooikappie*".'

I look at the picture on the desk in front of me. It's the same picture that's sat there ever since Koos came back from honeymoon ten years ago: his wife Lian on their wedding day. She has a sweet, innocent Afrikaans-*meisie* air about her. The bride is sitting on a suitcase in her wedding dress, in the middle of what seems to be a deserted road, smiling broadly at the camera. When I asked Koos why he's not in the picture he said a big, ugly Afrikaans man would have ruined the photo. I believe him. Lian looks complete with that suitcase, all by herself in the middle of the deserted road. A travelling woman always looks so beautiful.

'How is Mevrou Joubert?' I ask Koos. He smiles the contented smile of a man who has seen the same woman every day for more than ten years and wouldn't have it any other way.

'She's okay, just a little busy.' Translated, that means she's busier than he would like his wife to be. When I met her she was just coming out of her sweet-wife shell and on the verge of metamorphosis. She decided to go back to school and get an MBA at the UCT business school. Since then she has started a business that helps women entrepreneurs connect with the right markets, investors and mentors. The business is doing so well that she has been featured in local magazines and TV programmes.

'*Ag*, Maru man, I just want to have kids and get old with her.' He ruffles his brown hair and sighs. Koos just wants to have kids and his wife of ten years has just found her groove.

'Women are having children a lot later now,' I say.

'*Ja*, I'm not worried about that. Lian is still young, but I'm not.' He tucks his blue shirt into his pants and sits down behind his desk.

'What about you? Don't you want to have kids?'

Questions like that always make me nervous, because people give you funny looks when you say, 'No! I'm too selfish to devote my whole life to one needy little person. Kids are not something inevitable. They are a choice, one which I have decided not to make.' So instead I just say, '*Ja*, maybe one day,' and exit quickly before the conversation can get any further.

I make my way to my office feeling a wave of nausea rising. A melody creeps out of the corners of my mind and my heart jumps into my throat. I feel its pounding echoing in my empty head, competing with the song.

'*Bana be sekolo, bana sekolo …*' This is not a thought. It is not a memory. Nor is it something created by my imagination. It is the sound of children singing in my head as clearly as if I could pull them out of my brain and they would stand there, right before me in my office. Faces glowing with a Vaseline shine, all smiling proudly in their black gym dresses with crisp white shirts underneath. '*Tlong sekolong, tlong sekolong ...*'

I try to immerse myself in my work but I can't concentrate. Maybe I should call Unathi. I do, but her phone is off. My cellphone rings and the screen tells me that it's Ma. I'm definitely not picking up her call right now. If I hear any more stuff about weddings and family I might just kill myself before the nausea does.

Sometimes I wish Baba was still alive. I loved him before and after he became a snake. He always seemed to know the story that lurked behind my eyes. 'You are going to be stuck between green and blue one day, Marubini. The past and future will stalk you. Don't choose either of them, always choose today.'

He never used to say things like that to me, but after he came from beneath the water he spoke that way all the time. I didn't understand most of what he said. But I loved that he looked at me so thoughtfully, as though I was something special. He was all Red, White and Brown. Brown skin draped in red and white clothes and beads. I still miss him so much. Sometimes it feels like my mother has only just said those words: 'Baba is not coming back,' and I still cannot process that reality.

'Any plans to join us, young lady?' Koos's face appears at the door.

'Who's us?'

'Our reps ...'

'Do we have to do this?'

'Rep manager is on honeymoon, remember?'

'Oh *ja*. What is it with people and marriage lately?'

I collect my diary, phone and bag, Red, White and Brown swirling around my mind as I follow Koos to the boardroom where our reps are waiting for us. De Villiers Wines is one of South Africa's oldest and biggest wine farms. We sell more wine than any other farm in the country. Because of this, we hire reps who work all over the country. Everything is done in-house and the farm is still owned by the De Villiers family. Most of the reps sitting in front of me have worked for De Villiers for many years. While Koos tells them about the new market segment we'll be targeting and the training workshops that will be held soon, I sit next to him quietly.

He keeps looking over at me for confirmation that he is giving them the right information. I nod a couple of times; but I can't silence the song in my head. *'Bana ba sekolo, bana ba sekolo. Tlong sekolong, tlong sekolong. Utlwang tshepe e a lla, utlwang tshepe e a lla. Ding dong bell.'* The Sesotho words, sung to the 'Frere Jacques' tune, give me an instant headache and my heart starts beating faster again. I wipe my sweaty palms on my brown pants and surreptitiously squeeze the area between my thumb and index finger, as if believing all of a sudden that Unathi's silly remedy will cure me of this phantom hangover. Koos hands over to me after fifteen minutes of talking to blank faces. I take the reps through the profile of our 'new' target market.

'These are people who have been overlooked in the past,' I say and catch a girl at the back of the room, whom I recognise as Leigh-Anne, rolling her eyes and mouthing, 'That means blacks.'

I smile and look her straight in the eye: 'Yes, you're right, Leigh-Anne, mostly black people.'

The wine industry has never been interested in black people. While other alcohol brands were flooding townships with their bottom-of-the-range beverages, winemakers completely ignored the potential of the main market. At my insistence, after months of back and forth discussions supported by data from our research company, De Villiers has finally decided to go after the 'emerging market'. The great release of the black majority from the talons of white minority government rule and the inequalities of apartheid has brought about a lot of changes to this beautiful country. All sectors were altered and influenced by this long-overdue liberation; advertising, too, did not escape.

It would be wrong for me to pretend that major changes were not also taking place in the world of marketing and branding. No longer will De Villiers wines be enjoyed solely by the Judge Johans and Architect Steves in their mansions situated in exclusive suburbs or on the decks of their holiday homes and yachts in the Western Cape. This premium brand will now also be enjoyed and abused by a middle-class black market. Including *bo* Malume who has just signed a lucrative BEE deal, and *bo*-cuzzy who has come upon ridiculous promotions in record time.

I too am part of the history-making process as I stand in this room briefing our reps about the new target market and our plans for the future. The reps don't seem very interested in my presentation. A young guy in a salmon shirt and slicked-back hair is chatting on his Blackberry. The overweight older guy next to him is kicking the chair in front of him, much to the annoyance of the stick-thin girl sitting on it. I keep speaking and ignore the blank faces. A hand goes up at the back. 'Do we get to go on township tours?' 'Because all black people live in townships, isn't it?' is the sardonic response of the stick-thin girl to the questioner. Another hand goes up: 'Obviously we're not talking here about marketing the premium range to this "new" market … Are we?'

Koos gets to his feet with a smile. 'Questions later, *asseblief*, just let Maru finish.'

I would have been happy to indulge the conversation further had the children not chosen that moment to start singing again. '*Bana ba sekolo, bana ba sekolo* …' I end my presentation abruptly. The children don't stop their animated singing. All through the rest of the reps' questions they sing on, softly and playfully, as though mindful of not disturbing me at work. Fear pulls up next to me and holds my hand. I'm really, really scared.

'You don't want to go to crèche but you want to go to school?'

'Ea, Ntatemoholo. I like the school clothes.'

'Well, one day you will attend school but for now we just wave goodbye to the school children.'

My grandfather and I spent many mornings watching the school children walk to the school nearby. They looked so lovely. I could just see myself in the crisp white shirt and black gym dress with the wool belt that they all wore. Everything Ntatemoholo and I did was an opportunity for me to learn something. The plastic table cover in the kitchen had drawings of the 'Big 5'. I didn't know their names, but Ntatemoholo did. He taught them to me in English and Sepedi. 'Baaahfelow. Luhyon …' I stopped reciting and laughed at how silly I sounded.

Ntatemoholo had attended the mission school in Pietersburg, so he knew a lot of things. I always had questions for him and he tried his best to answer them. When he didn't know he said, 'I don't know, Marubini. You ask so many questions.' Then he'd tickle me and ask me questions that he knew I would have the answers to.

'Never be afraid to ask questions, *motoholo*. Things are not so scary when you ask questions.'

'It means something like, Preacher Jacques, are you sleeping, uh ...' Pierre sighs into the phone. My poor man is trying to translate something seemingly elementary from French to English for me. He continues to explain over the background buzz of La Cuisine: 'The morning bells are ringing and ... you know the rest ... Ding dong dang!' He keeps quiet and waits for me to explain why I have called him in the middle of a busy evening to ask him about a nursery rhyme.

'It's just something our agency suggested, so I want to check they don't do anything stupid. Thanks babe, go back to work,' I say, trying to avoid an inquisition. How would I even begin explaining to him that the reason he had to stop talking to his staff before the 'shop' started filling up is because there was a stupid children's song playing in my head? The Sesotho song is not so different from the original French one. The version the children are singing in my head invites school children to the school: 'School Children. School Children. Come to school. The school bell is ringing. Ding dong bell.'

I pour myself a whiskey and sit down to enjoy a burger and chips as I look over the agency's lacklustre proposal. Best to enjoy the finer things in life while I try to look for the good in someone else's work. Time passes quickly when you find yourself in front of your laptop. The clock on the right-hand corner of my screen says it's approaching 9.00 p.m. As I close the laptop I glimpse something moving at the edge of my vision. Did I see something? Maybe I imagined it, a smudge that disappeared into nothing.

'*Bana ba sekolo* ...' The song returns. Softer, but somehow more threatening for that. What is that lurking in the shadows at the corner of my eye? With supersonic speed it disappears into the wall. I whip my head around to get a better look. '*O mang? Ke wena mang?*' My frightened voice leaps out of my mouth, demanding to know who or what is lurking in the shadows of my mind and of the room. My sitting room is tormenting me!

The room begins to sway slowly. There's a dark spot in one corner, as if the light has suddenly retracted from that spot. '*Tlong sekolong, tlong sekolong* ...' A table ... No, a bed. It's too dark to make out clearly. The projection of an epoch long forgotten floats in the dim corner of my sitting room. Like a photograph rocking back and forth on the waters of a deserted river. Not seeking to be found or remembered but just floating there, following the currents of the water, not aware of its purpose or history.

The darkness smells like damp ... mildew, so strong it clings to anything within its reach. The elusive figure that I glimpsed earlier mumbles something that echoes for eternity. Young children become grandparents, waiting and longing to know when it will stop. Echoes, mildew, water, rocking back and forth without end. The mumbling has the sound of an old, tired cassette tape: slow, deep and distorted. '*Uzo hla* ...' The figure continues speaking but the words do not carry. We're so far apart, yet both of us are in this strange bubble of fear and confusion in my sitting room. Something is happening outside of this bubble that we are in; there are many voices, but the moment we are stuck in muffles the sounds and smells from outside. Who are they? What are they? A mob of them, indistinct shadows moving beyond the thin skin of the bubble. The room keeps swaying; confusion forces my heart out of my chest, filling my mouth. Slowly the warmth slithers out of my body ... '*Utlwang tshepe e a lla, utla tshepe e a lla. Ding dong bele-le* ...' Laughter. The singing continues. And then nothing.

A familiar voice reaches for me in the dark. 'Rubi? Rubi?' Another voice wraps itself around me: Pierre. I want to answer him but the darkness is so deep and invitingly warm.

'*Ke batla ho tsamaya* ...' That sounds like my voice. My hand is warm; someone is holding it. My eyes open and bright light sears me awake. Pierre is the one holding my hand.

'Don't say anything,' he says, kissing my cheek. My head feels as though a sharp ice pick was shoved into the back of it. I try to touch the sore place but Pierre stops me: '*S'il vous plaît*, don't move.'

The ice pick must be slipping out because my brain starts functioning slowly. I'm in a hospital room and there is a nurse walking out of it. A doctor walks in and smiles. 'You see, I told you she would be fine.'

'Fine?' Unathi comes round to the other side of the bed and looks at me as though I have risen from the dead. All three of them try to explain to me what happened to land me up in Chris Barnard Memorial Hospital. But all I can think is: thank God it's not Groote Schuur, I probably would be dead if it had been.

Unathi explains how she found me lying in a 'pool of blood' in my kitchen. The security guard at my building, who knows her by now, had let her in so that she could deliver her homemade butternut soup. Who does that kind of thing but Unathi? It was almost 9.00 p.m.!

After knocking three times and not getting any answer, her

default Unathi panic set in. She let herself in with the 'emergency key' I once gave her, and found me in the pool of blood.

In all the madness that followed Pierre was called from his busy night at the restaurant and I was rushed to hospital.

'You probably had a seizure and hit your head on the table when you fell,' is the doctor's verdict. The doctor continues talking. None of it makes sense, it's all just words: concussion, stitches, rest, cause unknown, seizure.

'Seizure?' Pain explodes in my head. 'But I don't have epilepsy ...'

'He didn't say you did,' Unathi says, looking at me fearfully.

'Not all seizures are an indication of epilepsy,' the doctor agrees. He stops talking and looks down at my chart then asks me the usual questions about how I'm feeling. I don't tell him how much pain I'm in for fear of having to spend the night in hospital. I couldn't bear that. Apparently the doctor is also a mindreader because he tells me that he knows how much pain I'm in; head injuries can be very sore and although the injury is nothing major I should try and get bed rest. The entire time he is speaking I am only half listening. Only one thing is bothering me: the shadow hiding in the corners of my sitting room.

On the way home Pierre keeps sneaking looks at me.

'I'm still here and I'm feeling much better, so stop worrying,' I tell him.

He doesn't say anything because he knows I'm lying. No words play between us for the rest of the drive. The shadow and the singing children have my full attention. Something in me wants to tell him what happened but how would I even begin to describe the song in my head, the figure in my sitting room? Everything is quiet now. I'm not even sure if any of it really happened or if I imagined it all, so I pretend to be asleep.

A very real fear is taking over the quiet in the car: what if I am losing my mind? Or what if I have a brain tumour and the seizures are making me imagine dark figures in the corners of my flat? Pierre breaks his silence only once I am home and safely in bed. My covers smell like fabric softener and I'm comforted by the smell.

'You okay?' It's something I should be asking him because he looks worse than I feel. Bags have suddenly formed under his eyes and the caramel covering his face and body is shades lighter than usual.

I nod and ask, 'You?'

'No.' He climbs into bed with me. 'You scared me, Rubi.'

Forcing a smile I say: 'It's probably just stress related, baby.'

'Don't make exc ...'

'Stress and the sharp edge of the table to my skull.' Another weak smile is all I can manage. Pierre smiles too and places his lips on my hot forehead.

'You should go back to the restaurant, I'll be fine here,' I tell him.

'No, I'm not leaving you. Why wouldn't you stay overnight like the doctor wanted?' I shrug. 'They can't force me to stay if I don't want to. Hospitals are expensive.' Not exactly a lie, but not the truth either. The truth is I hate hospitals. They frighten me.

Baba spent a lot of time going to the clinic and then to hospitals. The pain in his legs just started one day and kept getting worse. He stopped going to work because sometimes his legs would feel like they were on fire and he couldn't walk. If it wasn't his legs being paralysed by fire, then it was headaches. Blinding headaches plagued my father, mostly in the evenings. We would wake up early in the morning and take a taxi to the clinic. Baba didn't drive anymore because of the fire in his legs. Ma would hug us goodbye and get into a different taxi that would take her into town to her work. The hospital doctors didn't know what was wrong with Baba. The words they used were foreign to me. But Baba's face told me everything. The pills they gave him weren't working and it seemed the men in the white coats didn't know what else to do.

The hospitals we visited got bigger and the faces of the men in white coats grew more confused. Gogo kept telling Baba that he didn't need to go to hospital. She thought that she knew what was wrong with him. She said she had once suffered from the same pain. Baba ignored her advice and insisted on going to the doctors. We saw so many doctors that they all started to look the same. I used to call them 'Mister Doctor'.

Once, when Baba and I were making our way to Johannesburg General Hospital to meet another Mister Doctor, his legs caught on fire again. We were almost at the grounds of the hospital when suddenly Baba collapsed. I dropped the orange he'd bought me at the taxi rank and stared at him helplessly as he lay there clutching his legs, clearly in agony.

'Marubini –' his voice was stressed but his face was calm. Our eyes locked and I started to cry. '*Ungakhali.*' He held my hand and I tried to stop crying. He didn't have to ask me twice to find help.

I ran all the way into the hospital. It was quiet and cold and it smelled funny. There was always an angry woman at the front desk of hospitals, always on the phone; but this time there was nobody and I started panicking. What if Baba was in even more pain? What if I got lost in this big hospital and never saw my parents again? The thought of Baba outside on the road and me getting lost inside the hospital drove me wild. I started crying and a nurse appeared. She spoke in the same language as Mister Doctor. I cried even louder. Another person appeared. Everybody was speaking Mister Doctor and nobody understood me. I was pointing outside, crying and just saying 'Baba'.

A friendly young nurse took me by the hand and wiped my tears away. I pulled her outside and she followed. Her strides were too slow and my little hand tugged even harder. She saw my father lying on the ground and let go of my hand. Running and shouting she disappeared back towards the hospital.

Baba was still in so much pain. I sat down next to him. 'Sorry, Baba.' I tried to explain that none of the Mister Doctor people understood what I was saying. I looked up and saw that the friendly nurse was back again, this time with help.

That afternoon was not unlike many others spent at hospital: me sitting outside a room inside which my father was being poked and prodded. Then we would return home, having absorbed the cold in the hospital, and still without answers.

'Is that all the doctor said?'

'Yes, Koos. I promise.'

'Okay, just email me the documents and stay in bed.'

'I've been away from work for two days, isn't that enough?'

'Maru, it's a head injury, *dis erg*.'

'Okay, okay, but I'll be back next week, no arguing.'

'Okay. *Maar ek moet nou gaan*,' Koos says, trying to get me off the phone and, hopefully, back to sleep. The doctor thinks I should stay off my feet for a week and not be in a stressful environment. He has obviously never worked in marketing, otherwise he would have understood that he was in effect suggesting that I never go back to work.

My head is throbbing worse than ever and the stitches at the back of my skull make me feel the way I do when Nkgono plaits my hair. She holds my head between her knees and pulls at my hair, weaving it and patting as I squirm. I should call her and see how she is but she would know from the sound of my voice that something is wrong ... I can't make head or tail of this budget in front of me. The numbers are not balancing and I can't decide whether we really need any more above-the-line advertising or not. Maybe I should just admit that I need rest. The budget is staring at me; I stare back, then finally close the file and put it aside.

Simphiwe is in class, so I can't call him. He always cheers me up, my over-achieving little brother. There's definitely nothing on TV, nothing that I want to see anyway.

Ntatemoholo hated TV. The prospect of watching other people do what he could do himself or had no interest in really bored him. Instead, he would make us listen to radio dramas in Sepedi. He insisted that I stop doing whatever it was I was doing and come and enjoy the story with him. Those were quite possibly the best times of my life, sitting on my grandfather's lap and imagining the world inside the radio. Neither of us spoke when our story was on, not even when the adverts for OMO, Sunlight and Teaspoon Tips tea came on. All the big kids would be at school and the rest of the neighbourhood quiet, enjoying the moments of peace before the children came back and filled the streets with their shouts of 'Chicago!' as they jumped over empty stacked tins, or the boys played soccer with their makeshift ball made from rolled-up plastic bags and their equally loud shouts of 'Shibobo!'

Ntatemoholo would sit back on the chair and hold my hands throughout the whole story, almost as if to keep me silent because I always had questions about the intricacies of our story. As soon as the story ended he would say, 'Okay Marubini, ask your questions now.' I loved the fact that he never forgot to say '*story sa rona*' – it wasn't just another radio drama, or his favourite story, but *our* story: *story sa rona*. Ntatemoholo was the light of my life; he raised me.

I often wish that he hadn't died, and then maybe I wouldn't be in Cape Town, away from everything that I love and grew up around. I never felt the same after he and Baba both died. Although, if I wasn't here, then I would never have met all the wonderful people that make my life a continuous adventure and blessing; Pierre and Unathi being at the top of that list.

'Marubini, you have to stand here.' Baba bent down and looked at me. 'I know you want to see him, but children are not allowed in here.' I didn't say anything. Baba allowed me to caress the red and white beads around his wrist. Ma was already inside. She hadn't said much since Ntatemoholo was admitted to hospital. I had been sleeping a lot and was often confused. She was very short with me and hardly ever looked me in the eye anymore. Baba said it was because she was sad. I was sad too. Baba had come back and he was different. Ntatemoholo was the only thing that made sense in my world. Now he was gone and I couldn't remember a lot of things. Some days it felt like I just woke up and Ntatemoholo was gone and then other days I didn't know where he was or what had happened to him. Ma would get angry if I said I was going to wait for Ntatemoholo so that we could eat our food together outside on the stoep like we always did.

'You know he is in hospital. Just eat your food, Marubini.'

Baba let me eat with him in his hut that he built outside. The hut was another one of those new things that Baba had. Some mornings I would wake up on the floor of the hut and not know how I got there. On those mornings Ma would speak to me in a soft, gentle voice and explain: 'You fell asleep there last night.'

Nothing made sense anymore. I wish I could remember the exact day that Ntatemoholo injured himself. I had to stand outside the ward while the healthier patients were taking their walks in those bizarre multi-coloured robes that patients at Baragwanath Hospital had to wear. A man was wheeled past me, his face all swollen and covered in scars. Mama and Baba were inside with my Ntatemoholo and I was outside looking at sick and swollen people. The man on the gurney tried to reach out for me and I ran into the ward, past all the nurses who were too busy with their lunch to notice a little person running into a ward that children were not supposed to be in. I found my family with ease; Ntatemoholo looked like he was very tired. The way he used to look when my parents came home from work after he and I had spent the day together. It was a game we played, making my parents think that we didn't just spend the whole day playing games.

On seeing my face he tried to sit up but his body wouldn't let him. 'Ntatemoholo,' I said, suddenly so happy to see that old, wrinkly canvas that God had made only for me to love and enjoy. Every mole on his face was still where it was and his eyes were as young as I remembered them to be. I know now that it was the youth in them that I loved so much about his eyes. But back then I thought it was happiness or a joke that he couldn't wait to tell me. My grandfather's body aged but his eyes refused to. There was something that they wanted to show me about the world that his body couldn't. He couldn't play *diketo* with me on the stoep outside but we would play checkers in the kitchen while he was telling me stories about his youth.

'Marubini, *o batlang mo?*' Mama asked, in a cross voice.

'She's come to see me, just like you, Makosha.' Ntatemoholo reached out for me like the man with the swollen face had done, but I didn't run from him. Instead, I took his hand and kissed it. Sitting on that bed with my head resting on my grandfather's shoulder, I didn't know that would be the last time I would ever see him.

Grief is so elusive; just when you think the worst is over, it comes back again to remind you how empty your life is without the person whom you lost. In the days after I realised Ntatemoholo was never coming back home I was inconsolable and confused.

Mama thought it was time for me to start going to crèche again and be with children my own age. So typical of my mother; now that she had lost the one person who didn't mind being with me, she wasted no time in finding somebody else who could take me off her hands. She had work to go to and Baba was now a practising sangoma and couldn't always keep an eye on me. All his time was spent making medicine for people and seeing the people who needed his help. Baba could now speak to *amadlozi* and they helped him figure out what was plaguing the people who came to him.

So I was sent back to crèche, like nothing had ever happened. I didn't cry the way I used to. Most days I just sat quietly and watched the other children play or wandered around the playground aimlessly. Something was wrong inside me, but I didn't know how to tell anyone. The teachers didn't seem cross with me anymore. Now they looked at me strangely. Once, when Baba fetched me from crèche, one of the teachers said she was concerned about me. He explained that my grandfather had died and she nodded as though she knew what that was like. She hadn't even known Ntatemoholo but she was sad that he had died.

On that same day, Baba needed to consult with Gogo about something so we drove to her house. Baba was now able to drive again because there was no longer any pain in his legs. Going through *intwaso* and learning how to communicate with *amadlozi* had healed him.

Gogo was in her kitchen, singing and cleaning tripe. Her face lit up when she saw us.

'I know where I'm eating tonight,' Baba joked.

I slid into a chair and put my head down on the kitchen table. The two adults exchanged glances. Gogo looked very unimpressed. They walked out to her hut in the backyard where she practised. Both my father and his aunt had the gift of *ubungoma* and Baba relied a lot on Gogo to help him because he was still new at it. We went to Gogo on many afternoons so that they could discuss something that was confusing or troubling Baba.

I sat there waiting for them to come back. My eyes were heavy and I didn't resist the sleep that was coming on. Raised voices woke me up.

'Jabulani, please don't do this.'

'I don't have a choice, Mama.'

'What you are talking about is just a story. A crazy story! What if you damage the child?'

'Damage? I'm a healer. How can you say that?'

'You don't know what you're doing ...'

'Then help me ...' It sounded like my father was crying. Their voices became softer again and I fell back to sleep.

'Guess who?' A familiar voice from the other side of the door brings me back to the sofa in my apartment.

'Unathi, go away!' I shout, though secretly I am relieved that someone has come to see me.

Pierre walks to the door and lets her in.

'*Bonjour*, Nathi,' he says on his way out. Almost as if he's forgotten something he swings around, kisses me on the cheek and whispers, 'I'll be back as soon as I can,' into my ear.

'*Hai, suka* Pierre, go to work and leave us women be,' Unathi calls as she heads to the kitchen. I watch her glide across to the microwave to warm up something that she brought with her. Her long legs cover a lot of space and to get where she needs to be she doesn't need to walk so much as simply swing around left, right and left again. With that height and those legs that go on till tomorrow, she is perfect. Everything about her body is neat and poised; short hair, short nails, tiny breasts, non-existent hips (regardless of the fact that she carried the weight of a baby there five years ago). Unathi is long and flat from all angles, but she still looks amazing.

'Have you eaten, *wena*?'

'Yes. Pierre fed me before he left.'

'That weird French cuisine of his? No. I made you samp and beef stew for later, neh?'

'Okay fine, but I'm not hungry. How's the family?'

'Fine. I wish they'd stayed in Malawi a little longer, though. I got so much done when they were gone.'

'Your mother would have loved that, neh?'

'You know how she can be, Rubi.' She is smiling as she says it but I know that her mother's dislike for her son-in-law makes

Unathi unhappy. 'The worst part is that his family was so accepting when I went to Malawi to meet them.'

Unathi and William met while they were both students at UCT. He was one of her tutors and they fell in love very quickly. In her final year, Unathi invited William to meet her mother. Whatever Unathi had hoped for was nothing like what actually happened. As soon as William's nationality was discovered, he was thrown out.

'Never! My daughter with *ikwerekwere*? *Wena* Unathi, don't tell me I wasted all that money educating you only for you to meet foreigners.'

Things never got better.

A wedding and a grandchild later and Unathi's mother still thinks William is using her daughter for South African citizenship! The sad thing is that Mam'Wendy is not actually a bad person. It's almost like she attended a seminar where someone spread misinformation about the rest of Africa. She loves her granddaughter but doesn't think it's safe for William to take his own child to Malawi.

Another reason Mam'Wendy is upset with Unathi is because she got her degree and then decided to stay home. In her mind, she was sending her daughter to school so she could 'become somebody', with a job, money and all the things that she herself couldn't have when she was young. Despite the fact that Unathi is making decent money selling her custom-made bags and is happier than she has ever been, her mother remains unhappy. Perhaps she imagines the love of a foreign man is not as sweet or sanitary as that of a man from your own country.

Baba always taught me that we are all connected. He would say '*Singabantu*, Marubini. There are many of us all over Africa. We were known by other names before that.' I didn't understand what he meant then. But I do now.

'Rubi, my mother would love a daughter like you,' Unathi often says to me after one of their frequent fights.

'*Ja*, but I'm also with a foreigner.'

'But yours is not an African like mine.'

'Ha ha ha, his mother is an African, it's just that he has a European father.'

'I think my mother would still prefer *that* kind of foreigner.'

There are lots of things Mam'Wendy would have preferred Unathi to have done differently, one of them being the name she and her husband gave their daughter. William and Unathi both share a deep love for Miriam Makeba. While Unathi was pregnant she would sing the song 'Malaika' to her daughter. There was never any question as to what they would name their child. Mam'Wendy protested and asked what was so wrong with Xhosa names that had been in their family for centuries. 'What does Malaika mean anyway?' she said.

'I just can't please her, Rubi. And to be honest, I've stopped trying. I think that once I had a baby, I let that go. She will always disapprove of what I do and I will always do what I feel is best for my daughter.'

Unathi is happy just being what she is: a stay-at-home mom who makes handbags for people in her spare time. Now she is standing in my kitchen warming samp and beef stew for me, even though I have just told her that Pierre already fulfilled his duties as 'morning nurse'.

'I'm working on a new bag for you.'

'Me? But I didn't ask for one.'

'*Ja*, well, you'll like it.'

She walks towards me, holding two bowls of food. I decide to stop complaining because resistance is futile with Unathi. Instead, I accept the food graciously and listen as my not-yet-complete bag is described.

The day is not particularly beautiful but at least the sun is out and the rain has stopped. Cape Town rainy winters took some getting used to. In Jozi winter is bitterly cold but never cold and wet. Rain is reserved for summer as it should be, to help us and our gardens cool down from the brutal beating the sun gives during that time of the year.

'Are you okay, Rubi?'

'No,' I say honestly.

My 'day nurse' looks at me perplexed and says, '*Ku theni?*'

'I don't know, Nathi, I really don't.'

'I'm worried about the seizure that you had the other day. It's not like you to be sick.'

'*Hau*, I'm not a bionic woman, Nathi!'

We both laugh.

'How do we know that for sure? You have a seizure and then walk out of the hospital like it was nothing.'

'Uhmm, I was wheeled out actually. And I'm not unharmed. Medical aid is making me pay too much money for that short visit.'

It's good to know that some things don't change. After a week of 'bed rest' I am back at work and nothing seems too different. Koos and the De Villiers clan have followed my advice and given up on the search for an agency. Other than that it's business as usual.

Work may be fine, but Pierre isn't. He's calling more than usual and has started picking me up from work. 'What if you have a seizure while you're driving?' he says. I decide to let him drive me around for the week so he can see that I'm okay. It almost feels like nothing ever happened. Like the shadow lurking in the corners of my sitting room and the singing children never existed. Pierre is spending less time at the restaurant these days, which I don't mind too much. I worry that I'm getting in the way of preparations for his new restaurant opening. But it's fun having him with me in the evenings.

'Remember when you gave me carpet burn?'

'I have never given you carpet burn. I don't know what you're talking about, Pierre.' I take a bite of the pizza slice that's dangling from his hand.

'It was in Hermanus.'

'Oh my gosh, at the shocking bed and breakfast you took me to for my birthday!'

'It got a great review online,' he says, laughing and feeding me more pizza. I was supposed to make dinner but we ended up naked on his sofa. So we ordered in and remained out of our clothes. Pierre wanted us to spend time at his house. I didn't complain, because the shadow and the singing children may be waiting to torture me at my place. I still haven't told anyone about them. I want to, but who do I tell?

'Pierre, do you ever think you're going crazy?'

'Only when I'm with you.'

'Come on …'

'Crazy like how?'

'Like maybe you're seeing something that nobody else can see …' I stop talking and shake my head. 'I think I'm losing my mind.'

'Then … I'll help you find it.'

That makes me smile. When we first met, I didn't think we would end up here. All I wanted was a distraction; something to look forward to at the end of a long, draining day. Now here I am at the end of a somewhat calm day and I still want to be with him. He places his lips on my temple and I allow him in. It's a place he knows, an ever-changing place and yet it always feels like home. Hands on his damp back. 'I'm scared.' Head resting on my chest. 'It's okay.' Hands pulling my hips in. 'Yes.' Thighs squeezing him tighter. 'Yes.' Mouth around my nipple. 'Don't let me go.' Teeth grazing his shoulder. 'I want to give you more.' Hips moving in circles. 'Yeah.' Arched back falling into his flat palms. I'm scared of my own darkness. Cold chest against my wet back. Dive into me. Stroking myself. Moving away and crashing together. Legs quivering. Mouth open. Arms pulling me closer. We're both home.

The smoke in the hut was settling. Baba was carrying me, my left hand dangling. Swinging and bumping into the kitchen cabinets. He thought I was sleeping; my eyes were barely open. Maybe I had fallen asleep while he was working and I was getting in the way as usual. I would often ask him questions that he couldn't answer, touch things that I wasn't supposed to touch, but he would allow me to stay in his space until I dozed off or Ma called me inside. Words tried to come out of my mouth but my lips were asleep.

Baba laid me on my bed and covered me with a blanket. He said a few words into my ear and I fell back into darkness.

At some point in the night my body woke up before my mind could catch up. I was standing in the doorway of my parents' bedroom. The door was half open and there was a candle on the floor. My mind started waking up as my eyes fixed onto the candle. On the bed Baba was lying on his back, Ma was on top of him. Their nudity was the last thing I noticed. It was the tiny lights dancing in circles above their heads that had my attention. Their bodies were moving together in one fluid motion. The lights were changing colour: red, orange, yellow, blue ... Chasing the darkness away.

I didn't know what was going on, but something in me understood it. The lights started getting brighter until they became one glowing circle above my parents' heads, a giant halo around the naked bodies on the bed. Ma's eyes were closed, her lips curved into a beautiful smile and her hair was glowing. Silver, gold, platinum ... Her head fell back as their bodies were climbing and falling. Baba's hands and body were flowing but his eyes were fixed on the gigantic crown of light above him. Ma opened her mouth, let out a sigh and the light jumped into her mouth. A stream of it travelled through her like water making its way along a river to the ocean. My mother's body was illuminated; radiance moved slowly from her chest all the way to her toes then back up to her knees, her thighs, and rushed into the ocean.

Baba was the ocean, glowing beautifully. His eyes lit up in silver, gold and platinum. Ma threw her arms around him and they both lit up. Our house shook and yet none of us seemed to be afraid. I watched the candle go out, and then the light exploded with such force that it shut their bedroom door. My mind raced back to bed as my feet walked slowly to my room. Then into the darkness.

Pierre's breathing was slowing down. 'Where were you?'

'Uhmm, I'm pretty sure I was right here with you. I have the scars to prove it.'

'You just felt distracted for a while.' There is a frown on his face.

'I'm always distracted. I'm a woman.' The frown doesn't budge.

We eventually make our way to bed but not before enduring a bad C-grade movie on e.tv. It's a movie about a giant anaconda and a giant python killing people. The world becomes too small for the giant snakes and they hunt each other and fight to the death. I'm not sure if the death part is true because I fall asleep twenty minutes into the movie. And all that stuff about snakes being evil is rubbish anyway. My father was a snake. A water snake.

When we get into bed Pierre is not ready to sleep. He keeps tossing and turning. A book is taken up from his bedside, a side lamp switches on, and I hear him sigh.

I turn to glare at him. 'Are you serious right now?'

'I don't know why I can't sleep.'

'It's because of the rubbish you were watching on TV.'

'Tell me one of your stories, Rubi.' He is smiling.

'No, Pierre, I am not telling you a story.'

Another sigh. I roll my eyes. 'You're such a nuisance!'

When we first started dating Pierre used to come to my apartment after he had locked up the restaurant on Fridays. I would lie in bed and wait for him to call me. He would always whisper, 'I'm outside.' Once I had let him in, he would shower and ask me to talk to him until he fell asleep. I would tell him stories that my father used as a sedative for me when I was a child. Within five minutes, he'd be asleep. I would tell the rest of the story to my sleeping love. The stories were the only link I had to Baba. His voice was my own when I spoke those words.

Tonight, I begin telling the story that was my favourite, the one my father used to tell me when I couldn't sleep. The story of how he became a healer.

'You know, some people won't be happy that I'm telling you all this.' The regular disclaimer made the story even more exciting for me.

'Tell me, Baba.'

'Okay, but don't tell anyone else our secrets.'

He would get comfortable at the foot of my bed and start talking. The timbre of my father's voice was better than any cure for insomnia. It wrapped you up tightly and rocked you till you succumbed to sleep.

'Your Gogo told me that she was not the right person to look after me during my learning. She told me that my teacher was waiting for me. "Go to your teacher, Jabulani. Your spirit knows where you need to be." I had no idea what that meant.

'My mother abandoned me when I was a baby. She landed on her sister's doorstep one afternoon, with me in her arms. *uGogo wakho* says she put me down on the bed, while they spoke for hours. The two sisters had not seen each other in years. They squeezed five years into eight hours. Their hands cooked, their mouths sipped tea and allowed them to catch up. My mother, Zodwa, fed me one last time while her sister attended to a man who was convinced that his wife was making him sick. When the consultation was over, Zodwa was gone. She left without me or the bag she had arrived with. A bag that had only baby clothes in it. Nobody knows what happened to my mother after that. She had left home many years before she showed up on her sister's doorstep. Her own parents did not even know of my existence. I was an orphan, but only for those few minutes that your Gogo was outside.

'I had no idea where to start looking for the teacher that your Gogo spoke of. I took a taxi back to where my mother was from: Newcastle in Natal. Like her sister, your Gogo Thoko had run away from home at a young age to seek the fast life and fortune of Johannesburg. Her parents were still not talking to her. She worked in shebeens and eventually ran her own. But that did not last long, because she got the Calling and changed her life. When my mother followed in her older sister's footsteps and left home, it hurt her parents. My grandparents had lost both their daughters. Running away from home seemed to be a thing that many young people did at that time.

'I knew your Gogo wouldn't be happy that I was now seeking out the place where she was born; a place that for her had such painful memories and emotions attached to it. Somehow I felt that the answers I sought had to be there.

'Makosha said that trying to convince me not to take the trip was futile. She was afraid that I would be in pain for the rest of my life. Pain that only I could heal myself of. On the way to Newcastle my legs started hurting. I sat as quiet and still as I could in the back of the rickety taxi. A woman seated next to me offered me steamed dumpling and chicken feet. I had not brought any food, so I accepted gratefully. The road was bumpy and filled with holes. My neighbour screamed as the minibus swerved violently. One of the wheels had come off and was rolling away in the opposite direction. You and Makosha were on my mind the entire time. Would I ever see you again? Where was I going? Had I really accepted that the doctors could do nothing for me? Were my ancestors so cruel that they would kill me before I reached my destination?

'Luckily, nobody was harmed. The driver was a small, angry man who shouted at us, the passengers. In his eyes we were the reason his beloved taxi had broken down. An angry woman shouted back at him, complaining about the money that she'd spent and that she was now stuck between where she'd come from and where she needed to be.

'Something weird happened in all that commotion. I heard a voice. It sounded like it was coming from inside me. This voice was telling me to walk. I trusted it and just started walking, even though the pain was unbearable. How long or how far I walked is something I don't know. I listened to the voice and kept going. The pain in my legs was replaced with numbness. When my feet couldn't take me any further, I crawled.

'Scraped, bruised and thirsty, I arrived at the edge of a river. An old man was sitting there quietly, watching me fill my mouth with water.

'"Aha, a snake. I haven't had one here in so long."

'My thirst quenched at last, I tried to focus on the old man. He stood over me and instructed me to meet him on the other side of the river. I explained that I couldn't swim but he just pushed me into the river. My body felt like it was one with the water. With my hands at my sides, I allowed myself to move through the river. Not once did I emerge until I was on the other side, where the old man was waiting for me.

'"A water snake," was all he said. There were no clothes on my body and he was the only one of us who seemed to understand why. "Your feet are on fire because they are hardly ever in water. You're a water snake, you need water."

'My name, the entire time I remained there, was Water Snake. Some nights I slept in a cave near the water and waited for the old man to come and give me tasks. I started every morning with a swim in the river. The more I swam the clearer I became. In the water it felt like I had no lungs. There was no need to breathe or doubt myself. None of it made sense until I simply accepted it as my own truth. There are many things I cannot tell you, and most of them you wouldn't believe anyway.

'The old man told me I was a fast learner. He was a very powerful man and he was my teacher. One night I woke up to the sound of drums – loud, beautiful, hypnotic drums. I followed the sound. There were people gathered outside the cave, banging on drums and singing songs that my ancestors within me recognised. My stiff legs started moving and my body leapt into motion. There was nothing but me and the drums.

My feet raised dust and in that red dust I saw myself as I really was: filled with light. Beyond the light I saw other things as well, things that most of us don't see. Creatures that intended to steal my light. Disgusting, awful creatures; they were trying to hide, but I could see them. As the drums got louder so, too, did the silence inside my mind. My legs had never felt stronger, kicking up dust and waking up the ancestors. The ancestors communicated their wishes through my body; I was one with my source.

'One cold evening the old man came to fetch me while I was having an evening swim. "Come on, Snake, let's go and fix something." For such an old man, he really walked quickly. It felt like I was running to keep up with him. We arrived at a village, just as it was getting dark. He knocked at the door of one of the houses and a terrified man emerged.

'"It's starting early today," he said, moving hurriedly away from the house.

'"There is a *tokoloshe* that is terrifying that scared man," my teacher explained to me. I had become so accustomed to not asking questions that my fear subsided quickly. We went inside and sat down. There seemed to be nothing terrifying in the house that I could see; perhaps the man was mistaken. The old man sat down on a bench in the kitchen and started sorting the dried plants that he had made me carry. "We're going to burn these."

'"A *tokoloshe* that is afraid of smoke?"

'"Sssshhh ..." As soon as we stopped talking, we heard whispering in the corner of the hut. A sinister kind of whispering. Then crockery and cutlery started flying at us. This was obviously just a small, mischievous *tokoloshe*. It would have caused a lot more damage if it was truly malevolent. We burned some plants that I had never seen before.

'"Stay within yourself, Water Snake. These things can be very sneaky."

'What happened next was something I cannot explain to someone who has never experienced it. All I can say is, we spent the whole night trying to get rid of that mischief maker. It all ended in a stench. The worst stench you've ever smelled in your whole life. When we emerged from the house it was almost dawn. Some members of the small community were standing outside, looking terrified and confused. The old man gave the house owner some herbs to put in his bath water and incense to burn in his hut.

'"You might want to make peace with your neighbour, otherwise he will keep sending *tokoloshes* to your house." Those were the old man's parting words.

'"How did you know it was sent by his neighbour?" I asked, not expecting an answer.

'"The creature told me."

'"Why?"

'"Oh people can amaze you. They hurt each other and act surprised when somebody wants to exact revenge. Those who rely on revenge often don't see how petty and dangerous they are."'

There is a new woman at reception. The last person got fired. Although I tried to avoid finding out why, Koos had to tell me. 'She was stealing.'

'Why do we have to know this?'

'Because, Maru, this is where we work and people are stealing from us.'

'What did she steal?'

'Wine.'

'Who steals wine from a wine farm?'

Koos is amused by my question. 'The receptionist.'

We often entertain clients in the office, where we serve some of our wine. Meetings that should rightfully take four minutes end up taking hours. Koos thinks this is good for business, our clients wanting to spend a lot of time at our wine farm. Our meeting room is right at the end of the office building, where there is a pond and an unbelievably beautiful view of the mountains. On days when I don't feel like being at work I relocate to the meeting room. It feels like I'm on holiday when I work there.

Entertaining our clients includes serving them our best wine. Without fail there will always be too much rosé left over ('Men don't like pink drinks, Maru'). I had no idea anybody was counting those bottles. But it seems someone was, and traced the missing 'half empties' back to the old receptionist, Charmaine.

'I thought we all get the employee discount on our wine, Koos. Why would she steal wine?'

'Do you even work here, Maru? You never seem to know what's happening.'

That was the end of our gossiping about stolen rosé.

The new receptionist is Genevieve. She never really looks anyone in the eye and always appears slightly frightened. Koos thinks it's how all shy people are. Then why do I get the feeling that she's always looking at me from the corner of her eye? Suspiciously. Or as if she wants to ask me something.

On Fridays the office empties almost as quickly as the wine bottles we put out for client meetings. I could have also been one of the people making their way out of the wine estate before 3.00 p.m. But the time off that I'd taken means there are lots of things that need my attention. Genevieve is the only other person still in the office, sorting out her work space and trying to find her feet. She appears at my door. 'What do I do with all these open bottles of wine?'

'Did Nobantu not clear them away?'

'No. I heard Koos telling that young girl to go home and he'd clear up.'

'Well then, I say we have a drink. Might as well, if we're going to be here late.'

Genevieve scratches her arm and looks at her feet. 'I'm not sure if that's such a good idea.'

'It's just the two of us. One glass won't hurt.'

A smile sprints across her face. 'Well, my son is fetching me today anyway, so yes, I can have a drink.'

I stand up to fetch glasses from the kitchen. 'No, don't worry, I'll get the glasses.'

She goes out and my focus returns to my screen and the many unread emails I am crawling through.

I realise twenty minutes have gone by and Genevieve still hasn't come back. There are no sounds coming from the kitchen that is less than ten metres away from my office. Instantly my body tells me that something is wrong. The office is unusually quiet; all I hear is my footsteps.

'Genevieve?' My voice sounds weird in the silence. No answer. Then a big, cold hand falls on my shoulder. Something about the hand tells me it's not Genevieve. The hand dwarfs me instantly and a huge shadow is cast over me. I shut my eyes and breathe in deeply, telling myself that it's just an intruder and not the sinister stranger who was in the corner of my sitting room a week ago. The stranger is mumbling something but I can't make out what it is.

'Marubini!' That voice scares me and also breaks my heart.

A voice that has not been heard in a very long time, one that has ceased to exist, is suddenly coming from the kitchen.

'Ntatemoholo?' My heart carries my feet to the kitchen before my brain can question the logic. My dead grandfather in the kitchen at my workplace?

I run into the kitchen but there's no one there. Standing there, looking at the empty room, all I feel is confusion. I'm still trying to work it out when the floor beneath my feet starts spinning rapidly.

'Marubini.' I hear my grandfather's voice again but now it has a tone of distress to it. The light is slowly draining out of the room and the floor spins faster. I open my mouth to call for help but fail to make a sound. My knees give way beneath me.

'Ntatemoholo?' Hearing my own voice, I will my eyes to open. The ceiling appears above me and Genevieve's face breaks the flow of white paint overhead.

'Marubini?' She says my name perfectly.

'I'm fine,' falls out of my numb mouth.

'Are you really okay?' She looks strangely calm. 'Did you have another seizure?' The questions continue as she stretches out a hand to help me off the floor where I am sitting up in embarrassment and confusion.

'How did you know about the seizure?'

She says nothing and helps me back to my office. I'm not sure what to say so I look out the window. I do not want to go to hospital and from the way Genevieve is looking at me, that's where she's thinking of taking me.

'I really am fine.' That's me trying to convince myself. I don't need another visit to the doctor when he's just going to tell me that I'm having seizures, even though I don't have a history of ever experiencing seizures.

'Where were you?' I ask Genevieve.

'A man came to the door asking for directions to the wine-tasting. I was showing him where to go and I locked myself out, so I had to ask the security guard to let me back in. He said he didn't have a key, so I had to climb in though the meeting-room window.' She looks slightly thrilled and embarrassed.

She walks out and returns with two glasses, one with water and the other with wine.

'I overheard you and Koos talking about your seizures the other day.' She hands me the water and I take a sip.

'You need to take it easy,' Genevieve says, shifting my laptop away from me. 'Who is Ntatemoholo?' She says that word perfectly too.

'My grandfather.' She nods and sips her wine. We let the silence join us. 'You know, I wasn't sure I was going to get this job.'

'Why would you think that?'

A little more silence. 'I'm 45 and most companies prefer young people.'

I sneak a look at her. I thought she was a lot older than that. 'Where was your previous job?'

Her feet shuffle and her hand tugs at the jersey that is clearly too big for her. 'I guess you could say I worked for my husband. I helped him build up his company. But we're divorced now.'

'Like a PA or something?' I ask. Her lips attempt a smile but the creases on her forehead stop it midway. 'Yeah, something like that.'

'So how did you get this job, then?'

'My mom went to school with one of the older De Villiers

brothers. This is one of the few places where my husband doesn't know anyone or have influence.' Her body language tells me that she doesn't want to talk about her husband anymore.

'Who is the guy who picks you up every day?' she asks.

'My boyfriend, Pierre. He's worried I'll have a seizure and die or something.'

The silence is uncomfortable between us. Genevieve smiles awkwardly. 'Aren't you afraid you'll die?'

'Genevieve, can we please not tell anyone about what happened today? I really don't want to be stuck at home again. It's boring.'

Genevieve nods and somehow I know that my secret is safe with her. Something about her tells me that she understands what it feels like to have to question your sanity.

THE SON

S pring brings out the craziness in people. We, the sun people, stay indoors and sulk during winter. We're always in disbelief about how bad the rain is. Newspapers report on 'heavy rains' like it's a new phenomenon and people discuss the cold as though it is not a yearly occurrence. Once spring arrives, all windows are left open, braai stands come out, beach dates are organised and our wine estate starts receiving more visitors. Winter is when we do our planning, for our harvest festival, the famous 'Pinotage on tap' weekend, and live music events at the 'amphitheatre'. In spring Koos and I spend a lot of time talking to the press about what De Villiers wine estate has in store and inviting members of the media to our events. Koos lives for the excitement of spring and the extra work it brings. All his radio interviews are diarised in the shared office diary so we know where he is and when not to disturb him.

Pierre's business also picks up with the warmer weather. He needs more staff and training new staff requires extra time. Now, with the opening of his second restaurant drawing ever nearer, we are spending even less time together. I've resorted to spending my evenings having supper at the restaurant, doing my work while

I wait for Pierre to let Natalie do her job so he can come and join me. He tends to hover and has a hard time letting other people do what they need to do. Sometimes I can see Natalie rolling her eyes when he does this. Maybe he can see it too.

'I'm thinking of hiring another manager to help. We can't go on like this,' Pierre says, stopping by my table. I am sitting at my usual one in the corner. There are only two open tables tonight and Pierre looks pleased with how things are going. I haven't heard him sigh or use words that hurt, as he sometimes does when he gets impatient with the staff.

'Oh, but what would you do with your time then?'

'I'll think of something.' He's trying not to show that he's amused by my dig.

'I'll believe it when I see it.'

The idea of having a normal relationship for once makes me smile, though I can already imagine how upset Natalie will be; Natalie Kraitzek, Pierre's friend, full-time manager and part-time stalker. Everyone knows of a woman like Natalie, but few people can actually claim to know her. Not your average restaurant manager by any stretch of imagination. Average is something she detests and works hard at avoiding.

Born to wealthy Israeli parents, she studied at some of the world's 'finest schools'. She has a Master's in Fine Arts, and her paintings have been selling since she was in her second year. Her parents own a gallery in town. Pierre has dragged me to a few of her exhibitions. Mommy and Daddy Kraitzek aren't in love with the idea of her being a restaurant manager, but it keeps her happy. It doesn't hurt that none of her paintings sell for less than R40 000. When I told Unathi about those prices her mouth stretched open.

'Maybe I need to sell my bags for R40 000 too. Somebody must be willing to pay that money for a bag of mine, neh?'

Natalie and Pierre met at a mutual friend's engagement party. Pierre told her about his new restaurant and that he was looking for someone to help him run it. As it turned out, young Natalie had worked as a junior restaurant manager while she was living in Italy (different but equally interesting story). Pierre looked into her pretty brown eyes and agreed on the spot to hire someone he barely knew ... How trusting of him. They met for coffee the next day and hit it off. They have been close friends ever since.

'I don't want to disturb you. I'll come back later,' I said, walking quickly out of Pierre's office at La Cuisine.

'No, I'll always make time for you, Rubi.'

He obviously was not feeling awkward in the least about what had transpired the night before. So I put my brave face on and walked back in.

'Actually, I was hoping I'd see you tonight,' he said, in that sexy accent of his that sent immediate shivers down my spine. It made me think of the night before when I was in his arms and he was telling me how beautiful I am while tugging gently on my hair.

'Well then, I guess tonight is your lucky night.'

'Are you here with your friends?'

'No, just came to say hi ...'

Somebody walked in, breaking the web that we were weaving around each other. 'Sorry, am I interrupting?' the intruder asked with no hint of sincerity.

Pierre nodded and looked back at me. 'Yes, you are. Natalie this is Rubi; Rubi this is my manager, Natalie.'

The face that I always saw around the restaurant finally had a name. I'd had no idea that she was a manager. I didn't pay too much attention to her, to be honest; I only had eyes for one person at the restaurant. To me she was the girl who was always talking to Pierre. She only existed when she was standing with him.

Natalie gave a half smile and shook my hand. 'Nice to meet you.' She turned back to the man in front of us. 'So, how do you two know each other?'

The first thing that sprung to mind was the memory of Pierre lying naked in my bed, so I didn't say anything.

'We're dating,' was Pierre's response.

'What?' Natalie's answer echoed my thoughts.

I had no idea how Natalie really felt about me until about a month after I'd met her. I had spent the night at Pierre's house. He'd decided to take the Saturday off and I had a bright-spark moment, offering to cook him supper. I have no idea what I was thinking, knowing full well that I cannot cook anything worth mentioning. We emailed back and forth about the menu. I showed up at his house with a bag of Woolworths food, still not entirely sure what I was going to make.

My fear of looking like an idiot must have been very apparent. 'We' ended up making a seafood paella that put me to shame. Ntatemoholo had always cooked when it was just the two of us; he said I was too smart to have my head stuck in pots. It seems Ntatemoholo knew that I would one day find a man who would cook for me while I worked on wine-marketing strategies for Koos to approve.

The evening ended with Pierre and I having too much wine followed by drunken sex. I woke up to the smell of toast drifting up from the kitchen and a phone call from Simphiwe. He was excited about making the school rugby team. 'I'm so stoked, Rubi. Maybe one day I will be in the first team.'

'What happened to swimming, Sim? I thought you were on the swimming team?' He laughed. 'I can do both, don't worry.'

Sometimes I felt that Simphiwe was doing too much at school. '*Kanti wena*, when do you relax?'

'On weekends. When are you gonna come visit me again?'

'I don't know, Sim. Let me see when I can get away from work. Do you want Ma to come too?'

'Nah, I just wanna bond with my sis. Thanks for the money, by the way.'

'Anytime, *ntwana*!'

After my conversation with Simphiwe I called Ma to see how she was. We hadn't spoken all week and I was trying to avoid one of those 'so you ARE still alive' calls from her. Business at the flower shop was going well, but she wasn't happy about it.

'People are dying out here, *watseba* Marubini.' Ma told me how the funeral homes were placing more orders for flowers and wreaths than ever before. She was sad that so many people were dying of HIV/Aids. 'And it's all young people. It's so depressing ... even if it is good for business.'

After that phone call I switched my phone off and went to check on Pierre. As I was putting my slippers on I heard him talking to someone downstairs.

'What is the real problem?'

'I just don't know if I like her.' That was Natalie's voice.

'Nat, you don't know Rubi.' It gave me a jolt to realise it was me they were talking about.

'I mean I'm sure she's nice enough ... but I never see you anymore.'

'We work together, Nat, I see you all the ...'

'Is that all we are now, just colleagues?' It sounded as if she was about to open the flood gates on him.

Pierre was someone who avoided confrontation at all costs. Instead of telling Natalie that he wasn't interested, he would pretend that he couldn't see how she felt about him. He would let Natalie bleed herself dry, feeding the earth with her love, and never say anything. She had brought that metallic, leaking love of hers along with her that morning.

'No, of course we are friends.'

That heart she pulled out when she first met Pierre, I heard it drop. All that time they spent together, she with her hands stretched out. Offering him the heart that he pretended he couldn't see. He couldn't even see the pool of bloody love that she was standing in.

I felt bad for Natalie and Pierre's cowardice was annoying me. I didn't want her to say anything that would give him any more power over her, so I walked down the stairs as noisily as I could. Natalie stared at me incredulously and burst into tears. The only man in the room looked to me for an answer, but the only woman who was not crying could offer none.

I knew that crying of hers so well; not the tears of physical pain or heartache. This was the cry of shock, when something so unexpected happens it feels as if your heart might just stop functioning. So the next best reaction is to cry. It's a cry that shocks the crier more than anyone. This kind of cry does not respect dignity. Those tears will later embarrass and haunt you for as long as the memory of it remains embedded in your mind.

'Natalie, are you okay?' I asked, genuinely concerned.

She just sat there on Pierre's couch and cried her eyes out. When she'd cried the necessary amount of tears that healing demanded, she accepted a tissue from Pierre.

'I'm so sorry, I didn't mean to ...' She smiled at him sweetly and brushed her hand against his cheek.

Pierre's doorbell rang. It was a homeless person asking for food or old clothes. Pierre vanished thankfully, leaving me with his bloody mess. At that point I walked to the kitchen counter and picked up a slice of toast. Eggs that were meant to be scrambled for breakfast sat waiting on the counter. 'Is everything okay, Natalie?' I asked again.

'Mhhm,' was all I got from her, so I carried on with my toast task. In my butter-spreading trance I felt like I was being watched and looked up in time to catch Natalie's stare. I smiled at her, not exactly hoping to get a smile back, but definitely not expecting what came next. Her eyes were frozen on my face and without opening her mouth she said, 'I hate you!'

I stood there like a kudu caught in the headlights of a game-park 4×4.

'I'm sorry that he was scared when you were brave.' The words came out of my mouth, but I didn't even know why I said them.

She took them in but didn't say anything in response.

Pierre came back and Natalie was right as rain again. She apologised for being emotional and made an excuse about having had another fight with her parents about the same old thing, her choice of career.

That evening as I sat finishing up the presentation that I was giving the next day, I realised there were still pieces of Natalie floating around me. Her anger and resentment felt heavy in the room. It was clear that she didn't respect me or what I had with Pierre. There was something he had that she felt she had a right to. I had no right to him, in her mind.

Pierre was not blameless, either. I called and told him exactly what I thought of what had happened that morning. 'Don't apologise to me. Apologise to your friend and make sure that we never have to mention this again.' That was how I ended the conversation.

Natalie never spoke about that day. At least, not to me. For some reason I never accepted any of the food or drink she tried to hand to me. A part of me was afraid that some of her heaviness and resentment would seep into it. I knew that behind those smiling eyes was still the woman from that morning in Pierre's kitchen. The one who hated me because she couldn't hate Pierre.

'Did you hear that we are looking for a new manager?' Natalie walks past the bar where I am sitting waiting for Pierre. 'Now you won't have to spend so much time here,' she says through a smile.

'I will believe it when I see it. Pierre is a control freak.'

'He'll be busy with the new place ... It will be nice to have some fresh blood here.'

As soon as she says the word 'blood' my jaw clenches. I feel control slowly leaking out of me. My body is trying to float away from my awareness. Pierre appears and takes my handbag off the bar. 'I'm done.'

All the way to his house in Tamboerskloof, I feel like there is a fire stewing in my bones. Pierre wants to watch some UEFA game. I leave him to it and rush to the bathroom. The fire in my legs is getting hotter and there are sharp pains in my stomach. I run a bath of cold water and undress slowly.

When I lower myself into the water, the pain seems to subside somewhat. My jaw locks again but the rest of my body relaxes. I slip down further into the water and allow it to cover me completely. I am vibrating, pulsating. I have become my heart. Blood rushes through me, healing the fire inside of me and my whole body is pounding. The lights above me are moving as one with the water I'm submerged in. A black streak appears in front of me. Something dark and rancid is spilling into my bathwater. The black streak becomes a hand that wraps itself around my neck and holds me down in the water. Panic. The fire returns to my body, sharp and intense. I try to scream, but my jaw remains shut. Pain. The black hand is attached to a blurry image that is kneeling next to the bath. My feet are kicking violently. On fire. Water enters through my nostrils and sets my lungs alight. Fear. My hands fly about desperately trying to hold on to something. The black hand is still at my neck, squeezing. My whole body becomes a ball of pain and fire. I feel awareness slip away from me as I become one with the flames, until I am all black.

'Lebollo?'

'Yes. Now listen to me.' Nkgono almost never had my full attention. It was the consequence of being a curious child.

'What's lebollo, Nkgono?' I asked, looking outside at the goat I loved to chase so much. It was calling me to come and chase it. It was my fault that the goat was roaming around and sniffing at the fireplace where we cooked our evening meals. Nkgono would give me such a hiding if she knew that my little goat was roaming loose and not in the kraal where it belonged, with the other goats. Nkgono wanted to tell me about her job, but I really wanted to go and play outside. Why did we have to talk about boring things when I wanted to be outside?

'Marubini, theletsha.'

'Eya, Nkgono,' I said, wishing she didn't need me to listen to her.

My stay in Pietersburg wasn't so bad and I got to go home during school holidays if I really begged Ma. She had her hands full with trying to start her new florist business and looking after Simphiwe by herself. Mama didn't understand why I wanted to come home when the school holidays of different provinces were at different times anyway, which meant I'd have nobody to play with. Actually, the difference between my school holidays and those of the children at home wasn't huge, but I was a child and whatever my mother told me was the truth.

I didn't know why Nkgono wanted to tell me about her job at *lebollo*, whatever that was. Had I known that conversation would set in motion the most important events of my life, I would have been much nicer to Nkgono. I might even have called her Koko like she wanted me to. She was convinced that living in Soweto had ruined my chances of speaking proper Sepedi, and the fact that I used the Sesotho equivalent for grandmother, instead of 'Koko', was a perfect example of my 'diluted' Sepedi. She was sitting on the floor with her legs stretched out in front of her.

'*Etla o dule fa*,' she said and I promptly accepted her offer to sit down next to her. Nobody messed with Nkgono; if she asked you to do something then it better be done immediately and with no fussing either.

Our conversation had started off very differently to the usual. Nkgono was not shouting or telling me to do something that I didn't want to do; she was calm and spoke as if a lot of time had been spent practising what she was about to share with me. The sun was threatening to enter the hut that we were sitting in but the shade was winning the war. It was dark and cool inside our living area, which was not overcrowded with useless furniture or baggage. Everything had its place in Nkgono's hut. The chairs that were on the other side were used by visitors; she still preferred sitting on the floor.

'What is the difference between *nna le wena*?' she asked.

That's obvious, I thought to myself, she is old and I'm young, which was the only difference that I could think of. Nkgono laughed when I gave my answer so proudly.

'Yes, that is also true.'

The conversation moved on to what she did for a living. I couldn't believe what I was hearing. My grandmother taught young girls how to be women. That sounded like she did nothing at all. How does one learn to be a woman? What is the difference between a woman and a girl anyway? She also told me that she helped women have babies. I nodded, even though I didn't know what that meant. 'I have delivered so many children ... I've lost count.' Nkgono seemed pleased with herself. 'Then they get big and think they can talk anyhow to their parents. I have to remind them that I saw them on their first day of life and how happy their mothers were to meet them. Then they stop their nonsense. Nobody wants to hurt a person who thinks that your being alive is a gift.'

'Was my mother happy to meet me?'

I didn't need to look at Nkgono to know that she was smiling that broad smile of hers. 'Of course! Oh we were all happy when you finally arrived.'

That day my Nkgono sat me down and started telling me about the female anatomy and the changes that would take place in me. This was the conversation she had waited her whole life to have. A girl is like a seed; just the beginning stage of something big, something wonderful that will affect the whole world in ways unthought of, she told me. Many little girls grow up not knowing that they are the reason the world is still turning. Nkgono could see that I was listening but not fully understanding; she kept going, knowing that this was only the first phase of my education.

Morula seeds are pretty resilient but, like the rest of nature, still need nurturing. Under the shade of their mothers is usually where they grow successfully, but some mother *morula* trees have broken branches, or they have nothing left to offer. The fruits have been picked, the bark has been used for medicine and mother *morula* feels bare. So the baby seeds get carried away by the wind. They grow into trees all by themselves, far away from their tree family, without the proper care they deserve.

'When will I become a *morula* tree, Nkgono?' I asked, because I wasn't sure that I was ready to become a big provider of shade. But I was also excited always to have juicy *morula* to eat, whenever I wanted.

Nkgono was stifling a laugh. 'When the wind stops blowing you in its direction,' was the answer she gave.

Strong winds can take even the heaviest and strongest *morula* seeds with it. It is the elements around the seed that make it grow and become a force to be reckoned with. It is this process of growing that is the most important.

Nkgono now turned to me and pointed to my chest. 'That is where the first change will take place.' I lifted my top immediately to see if I indeed had buds that would later become leaves, then branches. My understanding of her metaphor was obviously a little shaky, but I kept taking it all in. Soon I came to understand the changes that a girl has to go through in order to become a woman.

'Is Mama not a full woman because she has tiny tee-tees, Nkgono?'

Again my granny laughed and said, 'Just as we are not all thin or fat, some people have smaller chests than others.'

'Nkgono, does growing hurt?' She rubbed my head and smiled.

'Sometimes.'

'Why?'

'Because sometimes we fight the growing up.'

A twitch, then a kick and some pain; I am filling up. Water is invading my body. I'm just a spectator. My legs start kicking till my head is above water. Coughing. A burning in my chest. The hand that was around my neck is gone. The noise in my head is too loud to bear, and I'm very confused. My right hand reaches for the towel rack on the wall behind me and knocks the wine glass off the edge of the bath to the floor. The glass shatters and a shard spins up and slices into my right wrist. I grab the wrist with my left hand to try and stop the bleeding, but I lose my balance and fall out of the bath. My left hand lands on broken glass and two big pieces pierce the soft skin of the wrist.

Finally my jaw unlocks and I scream. The blare of sound wakes every single cell in my body. Pain steps into me and I collapse on the floor in tears. Pierre's quick footsteps announce his arrival.

'Rubi?' He opens the door and gasps. 'What the hell?'

Blood, glass and tears silence him.

'I don't know ...' I cannot find words to describe what just happened.

He picks me up and carries me to the bedroom. After putting me on the bed, he covers me with a towel and stares at my bleeding wrists.

'How can you do this?' His face is angry but his hands are gentle, pulling pieces of glass out of my wrists and wrapping my wounds tightly with bandages from the under-utilised first-aid kit.

'Do what?' I watch him pace in front of my bed, cursing in French. I can only make out his silhouette; the pain in my body is blurring my vision. 'I didn't *do* anything.'

Pierre ignores me. He is busy calling an ambulance.

'Don't. I'm fine,' I whisper.

'Don't fall asleep,' is what I hear, but I can't actually see the man saying it to me.

'Pierre, I'm so tired,' is what I'm thinking of saying, but the words never reach my lips. There's too much noise in my head and body. Pierre puts a robe on me. No eye contact.

'Why are you angry with me?' I ask.

'What is going on with you, Rubi?'

'I don't know!' The words fly out as tears stream onto my hot face.

'Why would you try to kill yourself?'

Kill myself? Oh my god. 'No, that's not …' He looks at my bandaged wrists. I see the hurt on his face. 'Pierre …'

'I can't, Rubi, I can't.'

I know there's nothing I can do right now to convince him that I wasn't trying to end my life. I was fighting for my life. Against what or who is what I don't know.

'Why would you think I tried to kill myself?'

He doesn't answer, sitting with his back to me, breathing heavily. There are bloody cotton pads on the bed. The duvet cover is bloody too. I look at myself in the mirror; my lip is starting to swell. The mirror is misting up and the room feels like it's getting colder. Turning my attention back to Pierre I see the warm breath leaving his body, rising into the cold air … I can actually see it. I look around and notice that the windows are also misting up. Fear chokes me and punches my heart into fast-paced beating: The figure is back. I don't know where it is but I can feel its darkness approaching.

'*Tlong sekolong, tlong sekolong …*' Laughter. It sounds like the singing children are right outside my window, but that's impossible. Don't be crazy, Marubini, there is nobody outside the window. The singing breaks my heart and I have no idea why. There is something inside me that knows those singing children and wishes they would come in, so I can see them and they can prove that I am sitting on this bed. It's back again! The figure is back! I want to reach out to Pierre and tell him how scared I am but the figure is around, inside and over me. The bedroom is so cold and I'm fighting the shaking that wants to overwhelm me – I don't want this thing to win. I am here on the bed. *That* is real! I try to stand up.

'Marubini!' Ntatemoholo is outside, calling my name. The bed is swaying beneath me, bringing on sudden nausea. '*Utlwang tshepe* ...' Sadness and nausea invade my mind and body, hand in hand, happily playing a game of ring o' roses like the children outside. The agitation of the game inside of me is weakening me: a playground that cannot fight back.

'Marubini, *na o kae?*' I try to open my mouth to scream but a gigantic icy hand covers my face. Rubi, don't panic, this is not really happening. I close my eyes and the children carry on singing. '*Utlwang tshepe e a lla, utlwang tsepe e a lla* ...' I want to call out to them. Why are they playing outside while I'm stuck in this cold, damp room that smells of mildew? I open my eyes and Pierre is not there anymore. I'm sitting on a bed but it's not my own. The bed cover is olive and it smells like it's on top of an old, urine-stained bed filled with mites, fleas and ticks.

'Marubini!' My grandfather is outside. He is panicking, I can hear it in his voice. 'Marubini, *o ho kae?*' he asks desperately. I want to shout as loudly as I can so he can follow my voice and take me away from this monster that is covering my mouth. A hand-held bell starts ringing outside and the children stop singing. Their voices get fainter; they are running, running in the opposite direction. Then there is silence.

I am so scared that I start shaking. The creature is breathing on me. My body is trembling violently, but I won't cry. The creature is muttering, threatening me. My heart is crying for me. Ntatemoholo is still looking for me ... Don't cry, Rubi. My heart is crying harder, beating faster. Where have the children gone? The thing pulls me closer ...

'Marubini?' Where is he? Why doesn't he find me? My heart beats itself into exhaustion. 'Marubini!' The creature is getting angry ... I can feel it.

I try to get up off the bed; again the icy hand on my shoulder pushes me down. It's the dark figure and it's mumbling something that I can't hear. There's no more laughing or singing. The children outside are gone and it's just me in here. I am alone with a monster I can't see. Left all alone sitting on a bed that isn't mine, nauseous and terrified, afraid to move because the cold darkness reeking of mildew might harm me. I close my eyes and feel my body shudder from the cold. The shuddering becomes uncontrollable; I hug my legs and let tears roll down my frozen face.

'Marubini!' Ntatemoholo's voice resonates throughout my whole body; it shakes me like the hands of God himself were shaking me. My hands come loose from around my legs and there is stillness, warmth and silence. This is what peace feels like. I know because I've felt this feeling many times before: playing *morabaraba* with Ntatemoholo; sitting in the front seat of my father's blue Ford Cortina while driving at night listening to Anita Baker and watching, fascinated, the way the lights on the highway change the colour of my dress; Ma and I planting our seeds together and letting our fingers sink into the soil; the day Simphiwe said my name for the first time; Nkgono telling me her secrets in front of cooling coals with the sounds of nature all around us; the way Pierre looks at me, inviting me to fall asleep in his arms.

Waking up and seeing my mother's face is a bigger shock than realising that I'm in hospital again. I close my eyes, hoping that it's a bad dream. But Ma is still there when I open my eyes again. She is frozen in a pose: eyes sad, mouth smiling, fingers stroking my hand.

'Ma?' I whisper, almost as if saying it louder will make it more real than it is.

She kisses my hand and sighs. 'I was so worried, Marubini.'

I look around. 'How long?'

'Two days.' Pierre's voice eases my confusion. I turn my head to see him and feel dizzy instantly.

'Lie still, Rubi,' he says, putting his warm hand on my arm.

What could have happened that would require me to be in hospital again? How serious was it for my mother to have to come all the way to Cape Town? What if I'm dying?

'Why?' I ask. The explanation I receive is that I tried to harm myself and then had another seizure.

The word 'harm' makes both Pierre and Ma look uncomfortable. She gazes at her hands and he stares at his shoes. 'Harm' makes me undesirable and scary to them. They cannot stand to look at my 'harm'. The doctor said that I kept slipping in and out of consciousness for about two days. She still can't say what's wrong with me, despite having studied for all those years ... (this last part is my mother's addition).

The doctor comes in to see how I'm doing, tells me she's

concerned that I may have a brain tumour that is causing irregular brain seizures. 'We would like to do a couple of tests on you later today,' she says, tying her hair up. She looks tired and I feel sick with apprehension. A brain tumour? Fear is creeping up on me, first tickling my toes, warming up my knees and thighs before wrestling with my stomach and rushing into my chest.

'When can I go home?' I ask, my voice cracking.

The doctor looks at me and gives a non-committal headshake. 'I can't say for sure.' She frowns down at the chart in her hands. 'Let's just get the tests out of the way first.'

I sigh loudly.

'And I would also like you to see our psychiatrist, just for a quick psych eval.' The last part sounds very matter of fact.

'I'm not crazy.'

A soothing smile as she says, 'Of course not.' She goes out.

The rest of visiting hour is spent with Pierre and Ma trying to cheer me up, but I'm still trying to deal with what the doctor told me. Why would I need a 'psych eval' if I didn't try to kill myself?

'Don't worry about that now, my child,' was all Ma said. It hurt that nobody believed me.

Unathi called to say that she would come visit me that evening. I wasn't sure whether to be glad or not. I wanted to tell someone about the figure in my house, the one that lurked in the shadows and brought the chill of a highveld winter with it; about my Ntatemoholo who was looking for me, and the seemingly harmless children's song that was haunting me. But I didn't know where to start. I was worried that if people heard what I had to say they would think I had lost my mind for sure.

The garden was dry, my pillow always wet. Simphiwe was getting bigger and Ma was getting smaller. The nightmares were growing worse. Gogo told me that it was normal, but she didn't look like she believed it. Ma was off at work in the day and Gogo was looking after us. The school transport would drop me off at Gogo's house in White City and Ma would fetch us after work. She only drove when it rained; otherwise we took the taxi home.

Gogo always asked me questions like, 'What happens in your nightmares?' I would just shrug. I didn't know what exactly the nightmares were about, but I knew that I woke up scared and crying. When Ma came to fetch us, she and Gogo would stand outside, talking and giving me funny looks. Nothing was growing in the garden and the house was always quiet. I don't know how long after Baba's death it was, but one evening Ma changed my life with a few words. 'I'm taking you to my mother.' She had a weepy look on her face. The pap and chicken in front of me was my favourite but it went down like poison.

'I'm not angry with you,' she said, crying. I nodded and put more pap in my mouth. I wasn't swallowing, the food was just filling my cheeks. 'I have always wanted you, Marubini … I waited so long …' Food went into her mouth. A big gulp and then she continued, 'It won't be for long. I just need to make changes for us.'

'Is it because Baba isn't here?'

'Yes; all we have now is each other.'

'But I want to stay here, Ma.'

More food in her mouth and more tears; it was the most I had seen her eat in a while. 'I know, but you can't.'

Soon after that it was December and school was out. No doubt my teacher was relieved to be rid of me and my morning crying sessions. Ma had taken leave from work and we spent a lot of time together. She was trying very hard to appear happy. We even used the car more often. We drove to town to get new clothes and food while Gogo stayed with Simphiwe. Gogo called him 'umfana wam' – 'my boy'. Simphiwe was, according to Gogo and I, the cutest baby in all of South Africa. He hardly ever cried and he looked just like Baba. Ma was still wearing her black mourning clothes but her smile was slowly returning. We had been at the OK Bazaars in town, getting Christmas supplies. Ma wanted to do that before 'the blacks went crazy and filled up the shops throwing their bonuses away'.

When Ma spoke like that, Baba would remind her that she didn't really mean it and she was just angry. She often said things like, 'Black people are burning the shops in our own neighbourhoods. Where are we supposed to get food now?' Other times, it was: 'This stay-away is affecting our money. Do black people not know that the whites will fire us? Who will feed our children?' After Baba calmed her, she would look at him like he was the most wonderful thing in the world.

Most of our shopping was not for food but things that Ma knew we would need after the holidays. 'You know, Marubini, people always forget that there is a January after the December madness.'

I liked it when Ma spoke to me like an adult. I didn't really understand her words but I nodded like I did.

'They would rather buy their children Christmas clothes and lots of food and liquor … And then come January they are starving.'

She spoke like this until we were done with our shopping. I wished Baba was there to tell her that she didn't mean what she said; she was just frustrated with the crowds of people in the store. But the most wonderful thing in her world was gone.

When we exited OK Bazaars she smiled and said, 'I have a surprise for you.' We put all the groceries in the small VW Beetle and it felt even more cramped than usual. We drove out of town and entered a very quiet world, full of trees and smiling white families. When we got out of the car, I grabbed Ma's hand. We went into a shop with chairs and tables in it and sat down. A smiling man came up to us and said, 'Welcome to Milky Lane.'

Ma spoke to him. There was a mix of excitement and fear in me, but Ma acted like she was used to this world of milky pink chairs and staring white people.

'Baba liked the milkshakes here,' she told me.

'Milkshake?' I parroted.

The smiling man came back with curvy glasses filled with what would become my favourite childhood drink. We both got strawberry-flavoured milkshakes. Ma laughed at the look on my face after my first suck at the straw.

'Slowly, nana; if you suck too much you'll get a headache.' My mother in Mourning Black while we sipped pink heaven from curvy glasses; I felt Golden.

I spoke about all the people I would and wouldn't miss at school. She spoke about not wanting ever to go back to work again. 'I just want to tend my garden and fix the house.'

'There is nothing wrong with the house, Mama.' I wished we could be stuck in those sticky white and pink chairs forever.

Nkgono came to visit for Christmas and Ma was all smiles again. Nkgono and I didn't really know each other. I knew and loved her husband but she was still unfamiliar territory. That Christmas she told me about the day I was born, for the first time. It was a wonderful Christmas and suddenly I was magical; a child who brought the rain that revived my mother's garden. It rained that summer too, but the garden stayed dry and barren. I spent many afternoons playing games with the neighbourhood children. It occurred to me that they were all strangers. I knew some of their names but I wasn't part of the group. I was just a visiting ghost, tolerated but not missed if I wasn't there.

Ma and Nkgono had a lot to talk about and many people were coming in and out to visit. Ma baked a lot in December to make sure her visitors had something to eat. Nkgono made her delicious ginger ale. When it got too hot outside or I grew tired of the other children, I would sit on the stoep and enjoy the shade. Nkgono would keep me a plate of sweet scones and a glass of her *gemere* – ginger ale.

Gogo was also spending a lot of time at our house. She was slowly emptying out Baba's hut and making sure that none of his sacred things were left exposed. When she was finished burning things in the hut she would have lunch with us. I didn't enjoy eating with the grown-ups, so Simphiwe and I would sit on the cool stoep and have our meals. Every once in a while I would catch my mother and grandmothers looking at me strangely.

'Ms Khumalo, my name is Dr Duma Dubeni.'

We shake hands and I accept his offer to have a seat. 'Isn't there supposed to be some kind of couch here or something?'

The young doctor laughs and shakes his head. He tells me that he has looked at my files and spoken to his colleagues about me. They confirmed that there was nothing irregular found in my tests. All I had were bruises and stitches from falling and getting pieces of glass stuck in me. The seizures had no apparent cause. So here I am, sitting with the hospital psychiatrist.

Dr Duma Dubeni is probably in his early thirties. He speaks like he went to the kind of private school Simphiwe attends. He is a handsome guy; Unathi would give me one of her nudges: 'Hooo Rubi, did you see him?' I could just hear her saying.

'Dr Dubeni. I didn't try to kill myself. It was an accident.' I say this at the outset, hoping he will believe me. Surely his job is to tell crazy people from sane ones?

'A very serious accident, wouldn't you say, Ms Khumalo?'

I roll my eyes and shake my head. 'No, not really.'

'You have no issues with hurting yourself?'

'Please don't psychoanalyse me, Doctor.' I look up at him and see he's smiling slyly.

'I'm glad you are suspicious of me. People often come in here and pour their hearts out to me.'

'That's your job, isn't it?' His silence is meant to be encouraging. 'I feel like you're patronising me, Doctor ...' My voice sounds surprisingly soft. I'm tired and hurt. Even my own mother thinks I tried to kill myself. Something that she herself created, yet she accepts that it would self-destruct so easily.

'I am in no way trying to patronise you. Quite the opposite. And please stop calling me doctor. Duma will do.'

He puts his elbows on the desk and looks at me. 'So, ask me all the things you want to know about me. We won't talk about you till you feel comfortable enough.'

My back straightens suspiciously. What trickery is this? He seems to be sincere, though. And so I get to know him.

Duma Dubeni is the child of a woman who loved too much and an anonymous man who loved too many. Home is East London in the Eastern Cape, where his wealthy grandmother looked after her child and grandchild. Feeling smothered by the small, elite circle of wealth in the Eastern Cape he moved to Cape Town. The

University of Cape Town is where he became a doctor, father and 'almost' husband. 'uMakhulu wanted me to marry the woman, but life doesn't care what my grandmother's plans are.' He laughs a big, hearty laugh and I can almost see all his teeth. 'She met my bossy family and ran with her heart and shoes in her hand so that she could run faster.'

Somehow we both know this is not the whole story. I accept his half truth and he seems grateful. Who am I to expect full truth from someone when my own hands are holding secrets behind my back?

I offer him nothing about myself in return. Another appointment is made and I pick up pills from the pharmacy. The pharmacist smiles with pity stained onto her teeth as she hands me my prescription. I shove the pills into my bag and decide not to take them. I don't need pills to stop seizures or anxiety. What I need is to know about the black hand in my bath and the figure hiding in my house.

Our next session is not about Duma. He jumps straight in: 'So, tell me what happened on the night when you had a seizure?'

I shrug. 'Really?'

'Yes, really.'

'The truth is I don't know. I was soaking after a long day at work ...'

'Soaking in cold water?' My heart skips a beat. Who told him that?

'It relaxes me.'

'You don't want to know how I know that?'

'Does it matter?' He nods and I start building up an elaborate story. I was tired and needed a bath to wake me up. The day was busy and I hadn't eaten. I fainted and came to before I drowned. The glass broke as I was pulling myself out of the bath and it cut my wrists.

If there is any judgement coming from Duma, I don't feel it. It is hidden in the place where he kept the rest of his truths. A place most boys learn to keep for themselves once the world starts expecting toughness from them. Duma is an obviously tough guy. Played rugby at school, drinks whiskey and supports his country when it counts. The Springboks are playing a game today and he is wearing a national jersey to show his support. Mr Tough Guy has the softest hands I've ever seen on anybody and they are perfectly taken care of. His hidden place demands that of him. I suspect that it is this place, too, that compels him to care about the people who entrust him with their fragile state.

'It's important for you to grow properly,' Nkgono said to me while we were walking back home from school. Nkgono fetching me from school was becoming the norm. It all started after we had the conversation about seeds and trees. After school Nkgono would be sitting on a bench under the tree closest to the school gate with fruit in her hand, waiting for me. This was the highlight of my day until we started walking and talking about 'being a woman'. After enquiring about what I had learned at school and giving me a fruit, Nkgono asked me what my favourite game was. '*Diketo*,' was the reply that I didn't even have to think about.

Diketo is a game similar to Knucklebones or Fivestones. The aim is to scoop small stones out of a shallow hole in the ground while throwing a larger stone in the air. The players must then push the small stones back into the hole, this time leaving one of them behind, while throwing the large stone up again. The game really tested the player because none of this could be achieved by picking the pebbles up one by one; they had to be moved back and forth all in one scoop, while the large stone was in mid-air, because the player had to catch it with the same hand that they were shuffling the pebbles with. Once the first level, known as 'ma-dis-one', had been completed, the player could move on to 'ma-dis-two', leaving two stones outside the circle, and then 'ma-dis-three', and so on. I loved knowing that there was always something more difficult to come.

'Why do you like *diketo*?' Nkgono asked me.

'Because ...' was the only answer that I could think of. Grown-ups always asked strange questions. According to Nkgono, *diketo* taught me a lot. She said it was a game that helped me learn how to count and concentrate on doing two things at once. I didn't question any of my grandmother's observations on the game.

'I think it's important that you are able to play it.' A smile played on my grandmother's lips as my jaw fell to the ground and I almost choked on the mango I was eating.

'Then why do you always call me in when I'm playing?'

'*Ga o a swanela go raloka boshego*,' she said, explaining that children should not be playing outside by themselves at night. When I asked why, she simply said it was better to play *diketo* while the sun was up because of the visibility of the stones one was trying to pull out of the circle.

That was not the most important thing that I learned on that day. As we walked home, Nkgono told me that children must play such games because there will come a time when they will have to watch other children play. 'How will you teach others how to play if you've never played yourself?' she asked. I was already aware of Nkgono's style of questioning so I did not answer. Most of Nkgono's questions were rhetorical and giving an answer when you weren't required to meant that you were not listening but thinking. Nkgono didn't like it when I interrupted her either.

I was excited about my lesson for the day. As soon as we got home I changed out of my black gym dress and school shirt and went to play with my friends, to ensure that I would one day be a good teacher of *diketo* to some young girl who finds the game a challenge.

'There are experiences that shape who we are. It may be something small or big. Can you think of any?'

I laugh and have a sip of the water that he has considerately handed me. 'That's every single day of my life, Duma.'

'You know what I mean.' He has his 'doctor' face on. Doctor Duma doesn't laugh heartily. He may smile a little, and then carries on poking and prodding until he finds the place where your soul is bruised. Instead of answering his question I start telling Duma about things that annoy me. He listens quietly until the subject of my cousin's wedding comes up. 'Why aren't you excited about her wedding?'

'My mother thinks this is a very big deal.'

'Don't you?'

'Not as much as Ma does.'

Nhlanhla is the grandchild of Gogo's cousin. They moved to Soweto the same year I moved back home after living with Nkgono.

'Nhlanhla and I used to be close,' I tell Duma.

'What happened?'

'I was too different.'

'Why are you so sure that it was you who was different?'
'I've never been like other kids. What happened with Nhlanhla just made it clearer.'

Weekends were usually reserved for visiting various family members. The particular weekend that stands out in my memory belonged to Nhlanhla and me. The wheels of time were already beginning to turn a little faster for my cousin than they were for me. Mam'cane Mandisa and Uncle Johnny were going to a friend's wedding and they would have to leave us by ourselves until they came back late at night. Although we were twelve, I was very unsure about being left alone. My cousin, by contrast, was all excitement. She promised to look after me, like I was some kind of baby.

Mam'cane Mandisa rushed around the house, leaving a sweet mix of Lifebuoy soap and perfume behind her, making sure our supper was cooked, telling us to eat at 7.00 p.m., reminding us to close the windows and switch the lights on when it got dark. Malume Johnny was hooting outside; he was always in a hurry to leave. Nhlanhla helped her mother out of the house, carrying her bag and laughing at the way her father was hooting impatiently. I stood outside the car and got a brief kiss and 'You must behave, *nana*'. Nhlanhla and I stood at the gate and watched her parents drive away to the wedding in Atteridgeville.

The day progressed like any other day did. We went to visit friends of my cousins and talked while we walked around the neighbourhood aimlessly. After purchasing *ama-kipkip*, one of the friends, Connie, decided that we should take a detour so that she could go 'check' on her boyfriend. Boyfriend? This was news to me.

Uncle Johnny often threatened us with death if he ever saw us with boys. 'Boys are only after one thing, girls.' Uncle Johnny never said what that thing was, but we all knew. In his opinion it was our job to keep safe something that belonged to us, instead of relying on the boys to know that they shouldn't try to steal it. When I told Ma what Uncle Johnny said, she looked annoyed. 'Don't listen to anything Johnny says, Marubini.' She explained that boys were not stealing anything and girls were not committing a crime. 'It's your body and you will know when you are ready to open those doors. You're my child. Come to me when you want to talk about that.' If only Ma knew that I was not at all interested in opening anything for boys – or anyone else for that matter.

Connie was very excited on the way to her beau's house, which was not in our neighbourhood. The way didn't seem as long for the rest of the group as it did for me; they chatted away happily, encouraging Connie to tell them more about her boy. Listening to the story made me even more anxious, because it surfaced that he was in high school and there was a possibility that he was with a whole group of friends. Walking the dusty streets of Molapo, I was uneasy about what was waiting for us.

When we finally reached this high-school loverboy's house, I was certain that when we got home Uncle Johnny would be waiting there with his belt. The boy who answered the door was almost twice the height of the rest of us standing at the door. AND he had facial hair! Uncle Johnny's belt took centre stage in my mind. But Nhlanhla did not seem too concerned about anything except joining the male voices coming from inside the house.

Connie's boy said his name was Tebogo and he was obviously the leader of a pack of runts. Walking into the four-roomed house, I was almost knocked out by the smell of young male; a smell that didn't please me nearly as much as it tickled my companions. This seemed to be involuntary rather than conscious pleasure. I saw the change in their eyes before they even set eyes on the testosterone-emitting bodies. I ignored the fake politeness of the boys. This was nothing but a cattle show, giving the studs time to decide which girl they wanted to be with. They organised themselves in height order and the shortest boy got to talk to the girl nobody else wanted. I wanted it to be clear that I was not up for the taking, so I sat quietly between the second biggest boy and my cousin. She seemed to be loving the male attention; I kept looking at her like she was crazy. The words 'boys only want one thing' revolved in my head, and I doubted very much that Uncle Johnny would be happy with her giving it away so freely; if, that is, incessant talk was the thing that boys wanted, because words were flying out of Nhlanhla's mouth non-stop.

The sun was threatening to set but none of the people I arrived with were showing signs of wanting to leave. They were all enjoying drinking Lemon Twist and eating cheap shortbread. Connie's boyfriend's mother was out of town, gone to visit his sick granny, so he was not concerned about being caught 'throwing a party'. We girls, on the other hand, did not have the luxury of parents who were absent, and our parents would be expecting their daughters home soon. Even though my aunt and uncle were not home, the neighbours would be wondering where we were. The trouble with living so close together and not having walls high enough to shield out the nosey ones was that they always knew what we were up to.

'Nhlanhla, *ng'cela ukukhul'ma nawe?*' I said in my Soweto isiZulu. She rolled her eyes and got up from the sofa that Connie had sat on briefly before disappearing into one of the two bedrooms of the house with her young stud Tebogo. Safely in the kitchen, I asked when she thought we would be going home. 'Why must you be such a baby?' she hissed. The insult didn't hurt. It was how she said it that made me look at her funny. She did not use her usual 'private school' accent; instead, she sounded like her friends. It was at this point that I decided I would go home by myself and did not need a gang of silly girls who all wanted to sound the same and were far more interested in smelly boys to walk back with me.

'*Ke kopa* key.' I spoke in my calmest voice because I could feel the tears welling up in my eyes. Equally calmly my cousin gave me the house keys and dared me to walk home alone. Something inside me double-dared me to accept her dare. So that's what I did.

When she realised I was serious, she followed me outside and grabbed my arm.

'Please say I am at Connie's house.'

'You want me to lie to *abo*Mam'cane?' She must have lost her mind for sure. 'And if Uncle Johnny asks why I am ...'

'He is *my* father. Not yours. No matter how much you try to please him, he will never be your father.' My cousin was still holding my arm. I would have pulled myself free if my body had been strong enough. It hurt even to breathe. She knew I wasn't going to fight back or say anything mean. I didn't have a father anymore and that was the truth.

'You're so weird. I heard my parents talking about you. There's something wrong with you. I don't want you here anyway.' She let go of my arm.

On the way home I started thinking about how Ntatemoholo had abandoned me. I don't know why I was thinking such ridiculous thoughts, perhaps because my cousin's rejection reminded me of the loss of my first and only true friend. We always spoke about how happy we both would be when I was rich and famous and how much fun we would have seeing Africa and the world. No one understood me in the way Ntatemoholo had. If I confided to anyone else how I wanted to travel our lovely continent and see the world they would quickly tell me I could never do it or accuse me of not being happy with where I was. The only thing that really interested girls my age was boys and the changes their bodies were going through. Things I had already been educated about, not in a classroom but by Ntatemoholo's wife, Nkgono *waka*. My busy thoughts shortened the long trip home.

The sun must have set while I was walking and feeling sorry for myself, but the fact that it was now growing dark and that it wasn't safe to walk alone never occurred to me; my mind was way too busy. I hurried into the house and closed all the windows. I sat by myself, weird and alone, just like Nhlanhla said. Even the adults thought I was different and peculiar.

About two hours after I'd reached home Nhlanhla stood knocking at the door. On seeing my face appear from behind it she whispered, 'Are my parents home?' Suddenly her everyday accent had returned. I shook my head and she pushed past me without saying anything else. Her eyes were bloodshot and a sweet, spicy smell wafted from her. She went into her room, shut the door and locked it.

That day changed our relationship forever. Our weekend visits came to a painful halt. What had happened between us brought home to me that I didn't fit in anywhere. I had many friends when I was growing up but I engaged from a safe distance. A distance from which I could maintain the pretence of being who they thought I was, without ever making them aware that they had no idea who I really was. I've always belonged only to myself. I've spent enough time alone to really understand myself. Nowhere in the world did I see myself mirrored.

Ma and Pierre are convinced that the sessions with Duma are really helping. I haven't had any seizures since they started, or scared anyone into thinking that I was trying to take my life. Duma and I had to take a break as the holidays came closer. He was going to Mauritius with his mother and the new lady in his life. Doesn't he remember the barefoot woman who ran away from his family's control? Doctors really cannot heal themselves.

Simphiwe finished his exams and flew straight to Cape Town. There was no convincing him otherwise. Ma was back in Johannesburg; Nhlanhla's wedding was getting closer and she had lots to do.

'I don't understand Mom sometimes.' Simphiwe always called her 'Mom', like that was her name.

I put the bottle of wine back in the fridge and watch my little brother make stir-fry. He has been cooking every night since he arrived. Cooking is one of his new hobbies. I'm not complaining.

'Why do you need to understand her?'

'Nah, she's always talking about how Nhlanhla is this and that and now she is practically taking over the wedding arrangements.' Simphiwe laughs as he says this. I'm not particularly amused because I get daily updates from my mother on flowers, people who have invited themselves, and how my father's family is trying to drive her crazy.

'You know how she is,' I say. 'She lives for the moments that need someone to take charge.'

Simphiwe's hands stop moving and he looks at me intently. 'Has she always been like that?'

'No. After Baba died was when she started doing the whole Corporal Ma thing.' Whenever I mention Baba my little brother's eyes soften. He gets told how much he looks like someone he has never met, and it's hard for him. He is growing under the shadow of a stranger that he wants to meet so badly, and never will.

He turns back to his foodmaking. 'Makes sense.'

The stir-fry is divine. We talk about spices, TV chefs and how awful most of them are. My phone rings and it's Koos; he is in a panic. 'Maru, you won't believe this.' He's right, I don't believe it. Koos left his USB stick on his desk. On it is a major presentation. He just landed in Johannesburg and has a super early morning meeting.

'Why isn't it on your laptop, Koos?'

'I don't know, Maru. *Ag*, I'm so stupid.'

'Calm down. I'll go fetch it and email it to you.'

It is the least I can do. Koos had gone into protective big-brother mode. People at work were a little nervous about my 'unknown medical condition' that might affect my working hours. Koos was a trooper; he helped where he could and never made me feel like I was not part of the team.

'Thanks, Maru. I owe you one.'

Simphiwe wants to drive me to Stellenbosch. 'I never get to drive.'

'That's because you don't have a car.'

'But I have a licence, Ru ...' He's pouting.

'You can drive us back, okay?'

The empty building is not as quiet as I thought it would be. It is breathing and humming. Some windows rattle. The old fax machine beeps intermittently. Simphiwe heads to my office and switches the lights on. Automatically he starts investigating the space. Looking for clues to anything interesting he may have missed out on. Koos's office has a great view of the lake during the day. At night though, it's usually pitch black. Tonight the moon is fat with light. She is gazing broodingly at her reflection on the surface of the water. There is a light wind blowing streaks of silver over the lake around her. You can see the grape vines that lie a little distance away from the lake.

The USB stick is easy to find. It's lying on the desk, annoyed that Koos forgot it behind. I switch his PC on and enter his password from six months ago. Koos doesn't believe in changing his password. He gave it to me 'in case of emergency'.

Sounds come from my office next door. My little brother is opening drawers.

'I can hear you snooping, Sim.'

He laughs, 'I'm not snooping. Just looking around.'

A whisper comes from outside; maybe not a whisper but the wind. The wind has a voice and it's trying to tell me something. I finish emailing Koos and shut down quickly, suddenly wanting to get out of the office. When I get to my office, Simphiwe is at the door and he is pulling a funny face.

'What now?'

'I need to use the bathroom.'

'*Eish mara wena*. Hold it in.'

'What?' He looks at me incredulously. 'No Ru, that's not good for my prostate.'

'Oh now you're just making things up. *Phakisa!*'

As soon as he leaves the room a feeling comes creeping over me. It's not fear. It is yearning. A longing to be outside.

My legs carry me to the door, feet barely touching the ground. A voice is telling me to walk towards the lake. I am not walking but running. The moon greets me, illuminating my way. My body's voice guides me. I'm naked. Now the bottom half of my body is immersed in water. The lake is cool and I am heating it up with my longing. The woman staring back at me in the water is saying something. Words I can't understand, but I can hear them. I mouth her words and my hair lights up: platinum and silver. It reverts to black again and blinks between the two colours. Steam rises from the water and hangs like a curtain, shielding me. My eyes close and I allow myself to sink into the warm lake. Time is suspended and I am without doubt, fear or confusion. The body voice speaks and tells me to trust myself with the truth.

'Marubini, you must never be afraid to tell the truth.'

'Nkgono?' I didn't understand why my grandmother would suddenly talk about the truth. She always did that kind of thing. We would be sitting quietly, just enjoying the heat and then she would start talking about strange things. I had stopped chasing the goats that roamed freely behind our hut. It wasn't much fun anyway.

'If you don't like something, you tell someone.'

'What about school?'

Nkgono laughed and shook her head. 'Besides school ...' she paused thoughtfully and carried on breaking the mealie in half. I was fascinated by my grandmother's strength. She could break mealies in half, cut wood, carry heavy buckets of water and still manoeuvre that old truck that used to belong to Ntatemoholo. I wondered if she missed Ntatemoholo as much as I did.

'Nkgono, do you know where Ntatemoholo is?'

My granny smiled and started making a fire outside our hut. She nodded and looked up at the heavens where her husband was enjoying the view of the ones he loved the most.

'There is something he wanted me to do, Marubini.' My eyes were stuck on the fire that was slowly growing in front of us. When I first started living with my grandmother the smoke from the fire used to make my eyes water. But now that I was used to it, it didn't bother me as much. I was sure Nkgono did not need me to ask a question. She could talk forever without any pausing at all. A child's task in the world was just to listen. So I did.

'You have to tell me the truth.'

'About what?'

'Everything, otherwise it will eat you up.'

What did Nkgono mean that things would eat me?

'What did Ntatemoholo want you to do?' I asked her.

She stretched her arm out and stoked the fire. 'To make you better.'

'Am I sick?'

Nkgono shook her head. We braaied mealies while my grandmother asked me questions. Questions I would soon forget and leave to float away in the beautiful Pietersburg night.

It's a simple question and I want to answer it. My body is getting cold.

'Ru, can you hear me?' Simphiwe is sitting on the grass next to me. He doesn't say anything as I get dressed. I sit down beside him and we gaze at the steam cloud hanging over the silver bubbling lake.

'Did you do this?' He sounds neither surprised nor afraid.

'I think so.' Those three words terrify me.

'Are you like Baba?' He sounds hurt.

'*Ha ke tsebe*, Sim.' I'm still trying to figure out how I managed to heat up the lake.

'Have you told Gogo about this?' Simphiwe asks.

'No, but I think she knows.'

The cloud starts disappearing slowly and the bubbling calms to a few ripples. 'Did you pull me out of the water?' I ask, knowing the answer.

'Yep.'

I appreciate the silence as we drive back home. Sim has insisted that I let him drive. He is humming along to some song on the radio that I've never heard before. When we get home I make my way to my bedroom; it is a quiet audience to the sounds of the ocean.

Sim walks into my room holding a folder in his hands. 'Can I show you something?' I nod and he sits down next to me. 'I don't remember you ever living with Nkgono.'

'Of course not, Sim, you were a baby …'

'Yeah, but what I'm saying is, I've always had you in my life. All my life I've heard how much I look like Baba … but I think we're both like him.' He opens the folder and on the first page is a picture of my father next to a picture of Sim. Baba is a smiling young man, standing in front of an old grey Valiant. Whoever is taking the picture is telling him something funny, because he's grinning and putting his hand up to make them stop. Green bell-bottom pants and a shirt with nauseating designs, buttoned all the way up to the chest. His Afro makes me laugh.

'That hair is big!'

Sim laughs too. The photo was obviously taken in summer

because Baba is the colour of burned caramel. The photo pasted next to the one of my father is of Simphiwe. He has a towel around his waist and he's standing by the school swimming pool. Their poses are identical, and so are their smiles.

'Gareth was asking me to pose like I was about to receive a Gold Medal at the Olympics.' Simphiwe smiles at the memory. The rest of the pages are all of his art. He has always been a great artist. He stops at one sketch and I gasp. It's done in charcoal, but I recognise the glow of the moon on the lake that I have just been immersed in. I'm sitting naked on the grass, watching the steam rise above the water. My back is hunched over and drops of water are falling from my hair to land on my tired shoulders. Although you can't see my face, I know that on it is a mixture of confusion and pleasure. Simphiwe is in the sketch too. He is handing me my clothes. His arm is just hanging between us, waiting for me to do something. The vines beyond the lake are drawn perfectly.

'Did you do this tonight?'

'No. A few months ago.'

Neither of us says anything. We just stare at the page. He turns the page over and it's another sketch of tonight. Half his body is immersed in the lake and he is pulling me out of the water. We are both bathed in the silver light of the moon. My whole body is underwater, except for the arm that he's dragging me by. Nobody ever says that Simphiwe looks like our mother, but in this sketch he does. It may be the determination sitting on his forehead or the softness in his eyes.

'Did you know this was me when you drew it?'

'No, but tonight I know it is. These are all things that I dream or they just come to me, Ru. Until now, none of it was true.'

Gogo is looking at me sadly.

'Thoko, I don't want you doing this to my children.' Ma's voice is very stern. I had just returned to Soweto after spending time with Nkgono and everything was different. We lived in a new house in a new neighbourhood and nothing was the way I had left it. I started missing Nkgono and our cosy hut the minute I walked into the new house. The entire way home from Pietersburg, Ma was telling me how much I would love the new house. She had become a better driver in my absence, no scraping sounds when she changed gears. 'There's even a toilet inside.' Her face was different. She was different.

I thought I would like the new house and I tried to be excited, but once we got there I didn't like it. Ma made it seem like the best place on earth: my very own room, an inside toilet, a big bathtub to wash in, a fancy electric stove and a big flourishing garden. 'I even sell flowers now. My boss, Mr Andrews, helped me to put together a nursery.' I didn't know what that was. But she seemed very pleased with herself.

She wasn't lying about the garden, though. There was a small corner where she grew vegetables for us to eat, but most of it was flowers. Flowers of all different colours, shapes and sizes in our backyard. The house wasn't much bigger than our last one but the yard was huge. Most of the space was taken up by the garden. The flowers had some kind of green net material hanging above them and the whole area was sealed off.

When I saw the small shack next to the garden, I thought it was a replacement for Baba's shack. My mother gave me a funny look when I asked her. 'No, our family doesn't practise that stuff anymore. That's all in the past, Marubini.' What stuff was she talking about? I just wanted to know if some of Baba's clay pots were in the shack. 'It's all my gardening stuff in there ... pitchforks, small spades and all the other things I need.'

Gogo was very happy that I was back. 'We should have a ceremony for you, Rubi ...' Before she could finish, Ma interrupted her. 'Mam'Thoko, I don't want you doing those things to my children.' Gogo looked at me sadly and then smiled at Ma. 'What happened to Jabulani was a great tragedy but ...'

Ma told me to go inside the house and watch TV with Simphiwe. I sat on the sofa next to my no-longer-baby brother and listened carefully to what was being said outside.

'What happened to Jabu was exactly because of him being a sangoma and you know it!'

'Makosha, how can you say that? They thought he was from the hostel.'

'You think politics killed my Jabu? You think the ANC killed him because they thought he was an IFP-supporting Zulu?'

'*Kahle*, Makosha.' Gogo was trying to reason with Ma, but she went right on.

'They killed him because they thought he was witchdoctor, Thoko!'

'Witchdoctor?' Gogo sounded horrified.

Ma lowered her voice. 'These ignorant blacks from Soweto don't know the difference.'

'It was politics, Makosha. It was a hard time for everyone.'

'Politics didn't burn my husband to death, Thoko. Small-minded people did and I don't want my children to face the same ignorance now.'

There was silence. They walked into the house and I pretended to watch *Mina Moo* with Simphiwe. He didn't even understand what was going on, but he seemed very entertained by the talking puppets.

'I'm sorry. I know it was hard for you Makosha.' Gogo was trying to make peace. Ma was taking tea cups out of the cupboard.

'It was hard for all of us. I never wanted Jabu to follow the Calling in the first place but he insisted. I never thought I would lose him because of it.' The kettle started whining and I couldn't hear anything else. My father was burned to death? I didn't know this. Ma had told me it was an accident on the train. That's what she told me. What is a witchdoctor and why did people think Baba was one? I just wanted to go back to Nkgono. Everything made sense out there. Nothing made sense at my new home.

It was school holidays and children made it their business to wake up early and run the streets. Ma would be up before daybreak and she would head out to her garden. I would watch her from my window. With a flashlight in her hand she would do whatever planting, weeding or pruning needed to be done. Then she would get herself and Simphiwe ready for the day. My little brother, unlike me at his age, attended a crèche nearby. Ma used to walk him there in the mornings and then take a taxi to work. She was driving more than when I was last at home but she still preferred taking the taxi to work. Gogo would arrive just before they left and Ma would leave her a million instructions about the garden, and about me as an aside. Everybody was still getting used to having me there. Sometimes Gogo would oversleep and Ma would have to call her: 'Mam'Thoko, have you forgotten about Marubini?'

Then I would be left alone to wait till Gogo arrived. On those mornings Ma would be extra jumpy and tell me a million things at once. 'Lock the door and don't open for anyone except your Gogo.' I would nod. 'I'm serious, Marubini. Ask her to come to the window and make sure that it's really her.'

If Ma knew that Nkgono and I slept with the doors open on many nights, she would have been upset. We never locked our doors and they were only closed to keep goats and chickens out. I didn't tell her, though. I just kept repeating everything she told me.

Gogo always encouraged me to go and play with the other children but I only wanted to be with her. The other children made fun of me because I sounded different. There was no winning, really. In Pietersburg the children accused me of the same thing. So I preferred to stay with Gogo who didn't care what I sounded like. The time we spent alone went by very quickly. We had breakfast together and then it was time for Gogo to see to the garden. I carried water when she needed it and sometimes she would let me pull out weeds. That time spent getting dirty and singing songs with my grandmother always seemed too short. Before I knew it, Gogo would be telling me to wash my hands. Then she would make us black, sweet tea with a thick slice of buttered white bread. After lunch we walked to Simphiwe's crèche to fetch him. Once we were back home I had to bath myself, while Simphiwe spoke to Gogo about all of the useless things little kids did at crèche.

After I was dressed, time just seemed to fly. Ma would arrive and Gogo would either take the taxi home or we would all climb into the small Beetle and drive her home. It was still weird to see Ma acting so happy. She wasn't afraid of being close to Simphiwe anymore. I decided I would ask her about Baba, while she was in one of her good moods. Simphiwe was playing cars in the sitting room and we were alone in the kitchen.

'Ma, can I ask you something?'

'Yes.'

'Did Baba really die because of people burning him?'

If Ma was surprised by my question she didn't show it. She simply wiped her hands, put the dish cloth on the sink and sat down at the kitchen table. She sighed and nodded. 'Yes, there was a lot of fighting and some people thought he was a bad guy.'

'Who?'

'I don't know them, but they thought he was bad, so they hurt him.'

'Why?'

'Because they were confused and angry.'

'Angry with who?'

'The government ...'

'Who is the government?'

Ma laughed when I asked this question. 'A bunch of men who use us for money and leave us out here to suffer.'

What did these men have to do with my father? Ma's answers left me even more confused, so I stopped asking questions. She could tell that I was confused.

'Baba loved us all very much. This was not his fault. It was just a bad thing that happened to a good man.'

'Unathi ... you know I don't like surprises.' The blindfold is making my face itchy. 'Can I please just take it off now?'

'No!' She had given the same answer to that question countless times in the last fifteen minutes. Malaika puts her little hand on my shoulder: 'We're almost there Aunty Rubi.' Both she and her mother giggle.

'I thought we were going to just have brunch and watch a movie.'

'I can't believe you actually thought I would do that.' Unathi sounds genuinely shocked.

Every year since we met, Unathi has made a big fuss about my birthday. I don't know why I was expecting this one to be different.

Unathi and I had met during a Leadership Camp in our final year of high school. It was an annual event organised by the top girls' schools in Johannesburg. We were picked from our schools because of our leadership roles or academic excellence.

During those December holidays Unathi showed up at our home with a cake. Ma was amused. 'You must be very persuasive because here at home we haven't been allowed to celebrate Marubini's birthday for quite some years.'

Unathi holds my hand and helps me out of the car. 'Two more steps. Okay, slowly, sit down.'

When I remove my blindfold all I can see is Cape Town below me. We're on Signal Hill. 'Surprise!' voices shout from behind me. Pierre, Koos, his wife Lian, Simphiwe and a few other friends are all smiling at me. Unathi looks very pleased with herself.

'Got you! We *are* having brunch, see ... on Signal Hill.'

A birthday brunch on Signal Hill with family and friends was the last thing on my mind. But it is exactly what I need. Cape Town looks so beautiful and busy beneath us.

'How do you feel?' Pierre asks. He knows how I feel about birthdays. The real question is related to my mental state. That topic would invite back the crease between his eyebrows. So I just smile at him.

'I'm grateful,' I say.

'Okay, I'll buy that.'

'Thanks for the food. Everyone loves your food.'

He smiles briefly when I compliment the food, then looks away. 'It's samples of the dishes from Afreek.'

'Why so nervous? You should be excited; you're opening your second restaurant soon.'

Pierre doesn't answer. He's stroking my left wrist woefully. I should say something reassuring, but I can't. There's too much going on in my head. So many things I haven't been brave enough to tell him. Where would I even begin to explain? The thought of the singing children makes me shudder. *'Bana ba sekolo. Bana ba sekolo. Tlong sekolong. Tlong sekolong.'* We had a music festival at the wine farm's amphitheatre last night at which Koos and I had to make an appearance. Simphiwe convinced me to stay till the last band had performed. It was well after 1.00 a.m. when we got home. I was too tired even to take my clothes off. It sounded like the singing was coming from my bathroom, but I knew it wasn't. I just sat on my bed hugging my legs, waiting for the singing to end. My body was shaking furiously. The song only stopped when I finally blacked out. I took my prescription pills for the first time this morning.

My tongue feels numb. Maybe it's a side-effect of the pills. The doctor said it was similar to epilepsy medication. I know now that my 'seizures' aren't the problem, and I agree with Simphiwe: only Gogo can help me with this. Simphiwe said Ma must never know about me consulting Gogo. Nhlanhla's wedding is in a few weeks, so this medication will have to do till then. I can't take any more time off. This is our busiest time of the year.

Pierre's friend Byron brings me a glass of champagne.

'For the birthday girl. Because the man in your life didn't offer you a refill.'

'Thanks, Byron. He's the worst, honestly. I'm only with him because he cooks.'

He pulls me up, grinning, from the concrete slab that I'm sitting on.

'Can't have it all, Rubi. Come and open some gifts.'

When I get home I decide to call Nkgono. She sounds annoyed.
'Who is this?'

'*Nkgono, ke nna Marubini.*'

She laughs loudly. Simphiwe and Unathi, who are sitting next
to me, can hear her and that makes them giggle.

'I know who you are. I also know that today is the day you
brought rain many years ago.' I don't interrupt Nkgono when she
starts talking because this storytelling on my birthday is an annual
tradition. Every year my grandmother tells me the story of my
birth day.

'You looked like a tiny queen from a time long gone. You know
that's why I named you Marubini. Do you know what your name
means, child?'

'Yes, Nkgono. It means "Ancient Civilisation".'

'You look so much like our people from long ago. You were such
a beautiful baby …' She laughs again. I allow her once again to tell
me the story I know by heart.

'When are you going to come and see your old grandmother?'
she asks, when the story is done.

'In a few weeks. I'll come and stay with you for a few days after
Nhlanhla's wedding.'

'Nhlanhla *ke mang?*'

I have to explain, once again, who Nhlanhla is. She sucks her
teeth at the thought of my cousin getting married. After a full update
on everyone she knows, she asks to speak to Simphiwe. He laughs at
what I assume is Nkgono remarking on his changed voice. The one-
sided conversation goes on for a while. Then the soundtrack ceases.
He hands me back the phone, still grinning and shaking his head.

'Okay guys, I have to go now,' I say.

'Ooooh, Rubi is on her way to have some steamy birthday loving!'

'Shut up, Nathi. We're going to have dinner,' I say.

'Ru, did you take your overnight bag?' Simphiwe asks, running into the kitchen to hide from my death stare.

'Sim, I'm in a relationship. I don't need an overnight bag.'

I shut the door on their laughter and cheering.

I can feel him watching me closely while I'm chewing. 'Well ...? Don't keep me in suspense.'

'Pierre, I don't know what Moroccan food is supposed to taste like.'

'Just tell me what you think, Rubi.'

'I like it.'

Our voices echo in the partially furnished restaurant.

'Well you're the first person to eat here at Afreek. How does it feel?'

'I sincerely hope there will be more people at the opening than there are today.'

A smile plays on his lips. 'Happy birthday, my love.'

'When do we get to sample the wine list, *kanti*?'

The evening flies by. I don't even notice that it's well after 10.00 p.m. till Pierre's phone rings. He looks at it then hands it to me. It's Ma. The idea that she and Pierre have each other's phone numbers still makes me uneasy.

'Ma?'

'Yes, of course it's me. Who else would it be? You thought I forgot, neh?'

'You never forget. Why are you calling Pierre's phone?'

'Yours is off. Simphiwe said you were with Pierre. I want to be the last person to say Happy Birthday to my first-born child ...'

'*Hau*, don't tell me *le wena*, you want to start telling Nkgono's story about the day I was born.'

'Hey, that's my mother you're mocking, *wena*.' A silence, then she asks: 'How are you feeling?'

'Much better, thanks. The pills are helping.'

'So there have been no more ... problems?' What she really wants to know is that I haven't cut myself open near any major veins again.

'No problems,' I say. It still hurts me to think that at the back of her mind Ma believes that I tried to kill myself.

'Good. Happy Birthday, Marubini, your mother loves you ... She also loves her garden, so I have to go.'

'At night, *pho*?'

'*Ja*, this wedding has kept me very busy. I've been growing grapes and I don't want my vines to suffer. Who knows? Maybe I will start making cheap wine.' She laughs and says goodbye.

Gogo was in disbelief. 'Leaving your job for what now?'

'To start my own business.'

'Good for you, Kosha,' Nkgono said, smiling. It was my thirteenth birthday and Ma had just made her announcement. My mother was leaving her job to start a florist business. 'You come from a family of growers, Makosha. If I lived here in the city where people pay for what the soil provides I would have done it a long time ago.'

Simphiwe thought this was very funny. He sat at the table sketching the four of us seated there. 'Let's have cake,' I said, rolling my eyes.

'Not before I tell you the story of the day you came to us, *wena* Marubini.' Nkgono still insisted on telling that story, every year. I'd told Ma that I wanted to stop celebrating my birthday. She acted like I was out of my mind.

'What kind of child doesn't want to celebrate their birthday?' She knew the answer. Everybody knew the answer. I was tired of pretending to be happy on a day that broke my heart. It was because of what had happened on my birthday many years ago. My father was supposed to have brought home my birthday cake and present: shiny red shoes. Instead he was dead. He left in the morning saying he was going to get my birthday present. Ma had said she wouldn't be able to pick up the cake, so he offered to collect it on his way back from getting my gift. I had seen those red shoes on TV, in a movie called *The Wizard of Oz*. Baba and I had been watching BOP TV one Saturday afternoon when the movie came on. We were both glued to the screen. He filled in the blanks when I didn't understand what was going on. I spoke about those red shoes for weeks after I had seen Dorothy wearing them. Ma wanted it to be a surprise but I heard them talking a few days before my birthday.

I was supposed to be sleeping but I was watching them through the crack of my bedroom door. Ma was rubbing her swollen belly. 'I think our little one is sleeping at last.' She sat down on the sofa while Baba was making her tea in the kitchen. '*Yazi* Jabu, I think I found the shoes.'

'Shoes?'

'Yes, for Judy Garland.' They both laughed. I knew that was what they called me in secret: Marubini, code name Judy Garland. I had no idea who Judy Garland was but I liked the way it sounded. 'I saw them in a shop downtown yesterday. I put them on lay-by.'

Baba handed Ma the tea and sat down next to her. 'She's going to be so excited.' He rested his head on my mother's shoulder as she sipped her tea. 'She seems to be doing better these days.'

'Jabu, are you sure it's working?'

'I hope so ...'

I didn't stay to hear the rest of what they were saying. I wanted to climb into bed and dream of my shiny red Dorothy shoes.

Gogo was looking after me on the day of my birthday. Time seemed to drag. 'Is it time yet, Gogo?' I was wearing my favourite dress and I didn't want to go play outside. After bathtime Gogo tried to convince me to wear clothes I could play in. I told her that I wasn't going to play. I was going to wait all day for my parents to come home so we could celebrate my birthday.

'*Hai, uph*' uJab'lani?' Gogo said, shaking her head. She looked outside. 'I told him to get that car fixed.'

I spent every day of the school holidays with Baba. He worked in the back, seeing people who needed help and I played within earshot, which was usually on the stoep. Gogo offered to spend the day with me because both my parents would be in town.

'I don't see why school needs to close.'

I looked at my grandma like she was not well. 'Why Gogo?'

'Because if it didn't, you would be at school instead of asking me what time it is every two minutes,' she laughed. I asked her again if it was almost time. 'Marubini ...' She shook her head.

Time really dragged as Gogo started cooking my birthday meal. Eventually Ma came home. Gogo looked surprised. '*Kanti* are you not with uJab'lani?'

'What? No ...' Ma sat down next to me. 'You look so lovely, my girl. Come here.' I gave her a hug and a kiss. 'Happy birthday, *nana*,' she said, then frowned. '*Hai* man, where is Jabu?'

We waited till the sun began growing tired of shining. Gogo walked out of the house with a scared look on her face. Ma was at the stove dishing up my birthday meal. 'Let's eat first, *nana*. This public transport is so unreliable. I told Jabu to get that car fixed ...'

Gogo walked in with a man who often came to see Baba. Baba told me that the man had persistent warts. As soon as he walked in I stood up and went to stand next to Ma. I didn't want warts.

Gogo told me to go to my room. No complaint came from my lips. Grown-ups always think that just because children are not in the room they cannot hear anything. I stood outside the kitchen and heard my mother scream. Terror froze me.

The wart man was talking. 'I'm so sorry, *sisi*. I wish I hadn't seen it with my own eyes.'

Ma sounded angry: 'What did you see?'

'It was this afternoon on the train. I saw uBab'Jabu, we spoke for a while. He said it was his daughter's birthday. He had a cake and a plastic with red shoes and a few other things. He even showed me the shoes ...' Ma gasped. 'A few young guys got on the train. I could tell they were looking for trouble. I had already moved away from uBab'Jabu; I was talking to some friends of mine and the train was getting full ...' I could hear my mother crying. Then I heard Gogo's footsteps and ran into my room. Gogo walked into my room. I hadn't noticed the tears that were streaming down my face. She grabbed me and held me. 'Oh you poor child.'

'Stop clapping, Unathi. I take it you like the damn dress then.'

'You're the only woman in the world who does not like shopping,' Unathi says.

'The only one in the *whole* world, Unathi?' She starts laughing. 'You saw how long Simphiwe took to find an outfit for this damn wedding. He has the shopping gene, not me.'

I'm bad tempered. My feet hurt from walking around the V&A Waterfront trying to find an outfit for Nhlanhla's wedding.

'I can hear you talking about me, Ru,' Simphiwe shouts from outside the changing rooms. Unathi is giddy with excitement. I never go shopping willingly, much to her dismay. I pay for the dress and we head to Sevruga for sushi.

'I'm ready to quit this job of mine, guys, really I am,' I complain as our order arrives. 'We are so busy.'

'*Ke* December, of course you're busy,' Unathi says, placing a piece of sushi elegantly in her mouth. Unlike me, who always seems to be dribbling soy sauce or chewing on a piece of sushi that is too big, making me look like a hamster.

'Why would Nhlanhla get married in December, though?' Simphiwe says, shaking his head. At least I'm not the only one annoyed at having to attend a wedding in the busiest month of the year. Taking time off wasn't easy. Koos was being really grumpy at work. Around this time of year all he wanted was to spend time at his house in Hermanus with his wife.

Everybody is busy in December – the malls, bed and breakfasts, wine farms ... everybody! Tourists running away from cold Europe came to Cape Town to spend their hard-earned euros enjoying the beauty of the 'Mother City'. Afreek is keeping Pierre very busy; we haven't seen each other properly in two weeks. The long work hours are making me tired and the stress keeps me awake at night. The medication seems to be holding the seizures at bay but it makes me constantly nauseous. My favourite foods have started tasting weird. The sushi I'm chewing is no exception. I take a sip of my wine and it tastes bitter too.

'What's wrong?' Simphiwe asks me.

'Nothing; these pills are messing me up.'

He doesn't say anything but I know he's anxious that I haven't yet spoken to Gogo.

After lunch I just want to nap. Simphiwe, Unathi and Malaika decide to go and play putt putt across the road from my building. 'Good riddance,' I tell them, yawning.

'Come on Aunty Ru, I'm gonna beat you,' Malaika says, smiling broadly.

Unathi laughs. 'You know your Aunt Ru is a sore loser. Let's go, Malaika. You can beat *bhut'* Simphiwe instead.'

They leave and I fall asleep on my sofa. The sliding door is open but the windows were closed all morning and it's hot in the apartment. The crashing sound of waves lulls me to sleep.

I am walking barefoot at the wine farm. The vines are disappearing as I walk past them. So are the new buildings; only the office remains. The office is where the original De Villiers family used to live. It's an old Cape Dutch house, recently renovated. But the building looks different today. The paint is off-white and chipping and there is smoke coming from the chimney. I sit on the grass facing the house, letting my feet slip into the lake. A young girl walks past me and eyes me nervously.

'It's okay,' I say.

She picks up a stick and pokes me with it. 'Baas de Villiers will be very cross that you are here.' Her finger points to what I know as the office.

A man emerges from the house and the little girl runs away.

The man is speaking in French to a small boy sitting on the stoep. The boy responds in Dutch. They don't seem to notice me; something is bothering the little boy and the man is looking for the cause in his eyes.

A naked old woman sits down next to me. 'We lived here all our lives and these French men get farms and us as slaves.' She bares her few remaining teeth at me. 'What are you doing here?' she asks, rattling the chains around her ankles. My shrug angers her. 'What are you doing here? This is our place!' She scratches my arm with long, hard nails. 'Tell them!' she says pointing to the man and boy on the other side of the lake.

'*Banna ba sekolo, bana ba sekolo* ...' Children are singing in the distance. I clutch my bleeding arm and walk back the way I came. Beyond the vines I see a school that I recognise. It is the school that children in my old neighbourhood used to attend. The school Ntatemoholo and I would walk past when we went to the shop together. The children continue their singing: '... *utlwang tshepe e a lla, ding dong bell.*' It's a small group of girls that is singing, but they sound like a choir, beautiful two-part harmonies and impeccable timing. When I get to the gate the school bell rings and they run back to the quad.

I want to speak to them, but my voice is stuck in my throat and they cannot hear me calling out to them. 'Hey! *Mtana ka Jabu!*' Someone is calling me. I turn around and the sun disappears behind green clouds. There is nobody there. All the lights are on in the four-roomed matchbox houses in front of the school. It seems everyone is indoors.

An old woman appears at the window of one of the houses. She is holding the curtain aside with one hand and pointing at me with the other. Her lips are moving but I can't hear her words. Her face has the shape of fear. The movement of her mouth tells me she is shouting. She is motioning to me to come to her. I can see her eyes wide with fear, the curtain shivering beside her. My feet start moving towards her and her hand stops motioning and falls onto her chest. My left foot is in mid-air when a big, cold hand slides around my shoulders. Deep down inside, I know that the hand and I are well acquainted. It was black ink when it held me down beneath the water in my bathtub. It reeked of mildew in the corners of my apartment. I open my mouth to scream but the hand covers my mouth. The creature grabs me around the waist. The floor is running from me as the green sky falls towards my head. I am being carried away.

Rubi!' Simphiwe's face breaks through the green clouds. I only realise I've been screaming once he gets me to stop kicking and scratching. My face is wet with tears and the air around me is thin.

'It's okay.'

I sit up and look at my shaking hands.

'It's okay.' Simphiwe keeps repeating this until I stop shaking.

'I was having a nightmare ... There were people ... children ... an old woman ...' My brother holds me as I cry.

'It's okay, Ru.' I hear him sigh.

We don't say anything for a while, but I can sense Simphiwe wants to speak. I look at him and widen my eyes; he knows this is an invitation to share what's on his mind.

'I've always enjoyed sketching, you know that. But a few weeks ago at school, I started sketching things that I knew weren't just from my imagination. When I saw you by the lake at the wine farm … it was like my drawing come to life. I was scared. But not anymore.' More silence. 'You always made Baba sound like such a wonderful person. Someone who wasn't afraid to face the unknown. You're facing something scary, I get it. But I think you're fighting this thing too hard, whatever it is …'

'I'm not fighting, Sim …'

He holds his arm up, revealing the bleeding scratch marks where I'd raked him. 'You need to find out what these dreams and seizures of yours are trying to tell you. They won't stop till you do.'

'What do you think your drawings are trying to tell you?'

Simphiwe shrugs his broad shoulders. 'All I know is that most of them are about you … So maybe I'm here to help you.'

I look at my little brother. He looks exactly like Baba, even down to the freckles. Simphiwe isn't little anymore. Here we are, me falling apart and him offering to help me. Everything that has happened scares me, but he seems just to accept it. Ma is not going to like any of this.

'Do you want me to show you some more sketches?'

I take his arm to stop him from getting up. 'Not yet, Sim. I'm not ready … Can we just keep this between us?' He nods and stays silent for a few minutes. The dimple on the left side of his mouth tells me he has something to confess: 'I don't think you were trying to kill yourself.'

'Thanks … You're probably the only one who believes me.'

Ma has been calling me more often, to 'check up' on me. Unathi just pretends that the whole incident didn't happen. It's the way Pierre looks at me that hurts the most. As if I'm suddenly something he doesn't understand or recognise. He isn't doing it on purpose, I know that, but it still hurts.

A crease forms on Simphiwe's forehead, indicating that he has more to say and I'm not going to like it. 'I'm afraid that it *will* eventually kill you, though.'

THE HOLY SPIRIT

'**M**y mother is Moroccan and my dad is French. Your turn.' Pierre was pouring wine into my glass.

'My mother is Mopedi and my dad is umZulu.' I held my hand over the glass. 'No more wine please ... Unless you are trying to get me drunk?'

Pierre winked at me. 'Why not? You can spend the night if you like.'

I laughed and shook my head.

'First boyfriend?'

I covered my face. 'Oh no! Why did I agree to this Q&A of yours? Let's talk about something else.'

'I'll go first. My first was my next-door neighbour, Edith. I was so terrible with girls. We were ten and one day when we were riding our bicycles she told me she liked me.'

'Go girl!'

He waited, smiling, for me to stop clapping and laughing. 'We dated till I was fourteen and my dad and I moved to Portugal for a while.'

'My first boyfriend was a kid I went to convent school with. His name was Kagiso. We kissed at one of those school disco things and it lasted all of two terms.'

'That's awful,' Pierre said mockingly.

'What is the most valuable thing your mother taught you?'

'That's easy. She taught me how to cook. That's where my love for food comes from. She met my father in Morocco where he was stationed as a pilot. She was an orphan and he was a lonely man. They became each other's family. My dad tells me that she cooked for him on their first date and he fell in love instantly. When I was born, I accepted that my mother was the best cook in the world. It wasn't just Moroccan food that she was queen of. She was sultana of food. When we lived in France, she immersed herself in the French cuisine. I wish she had lived long enough to come to Portugal with us ...'

The silence between us said that I wanted to ask but didn't want to seem nosy.

Pierre answered. 'She died of cancer in France ... What did your mother teach you?'

I told Pierre about my mother the florist. 'She taught me how to rely on myself, regardless of how little I had. Simphiwe and I were born in a four-roomed house, but my mother's hard work changed that. I witnessed with my own eyes how she turned a few flower orders into a thriving business. Her perseverance and love for plants put me through school. And as soon as I started working, I helped Ma put Simphiwe through school.'

'You pay for your brother's school fees?'

'Yes. It's an expensive boarding school in KwaZulu-Natal. Simphiwe begged Ma for ages to send him to boarding school. It wouldn't make sense not to help.'

Pierre stood up and started clearing the table. 'I think it's time for dessert.'

'What is it?'

He smiles his beautiful smile. 'A surprise.'

THE YEARNING

I had not met Nhlanhla's partner until I saw him on the Friday of the African Wedding. Gogo had called him *'ikhehla'* every time we spoke on the phone. I assumed she meant it in the colloquial way of referring to someone's boyfriend. But when I saw him it became clear that she meant it in the 'he is an old guy' way. Cows were slaughtered, gifts were exchanged between the families, and the newly married couple did the obligatory 'i-step' down the street for all in the neighbourhood to see.

Mam'cane Mandisa was very proud of her son-in-law, who looked like he was a 'better candidate to be her boyfriend than a son-in-law' (in Gogo's words). Ma was not as disapproving as my grandmother Thoko. Ma kept commenting how lovely it was that Cedrick had not abandoned his culture even though he was a multi-millionaire. Cedrick was 'involved somehow' in mining; that was all Ma could tell us about him.

Pierre was completely enamoured with the African Wedding event. He kept asking Gogo questions about the traditional clothes Nhlanhla was wearing and she was only too happy to explain everything. The wedding ceremony on Friday went on until the early hours of Saturday morning. Nhlanhla tried her best to make me feel included. Every time I stepped away to check on Pierre she would send one of her friends to come and look for me. I shouldn't have been concerned about Pierre because he was outside with the men, eating freshly slaughtered meat and drinking traditional beer. His cheeks and eyes were the colour of blood from the smoke and alcohol.

'He is going to get so drunk, *skepsel sa modimo*,' I said as Ma took me by the hand to lead me back to my cousin.

'It's a wedding. Let him indulge,' she told me with laughter in her voice.

Nhlanhla's friends were all married. I had to answer the inevitable question, 'When are you getting married?' so many times and listen to, 'Aren't you scared he will meet someone else?' so often it made me want to scream. Perhaps they had all rehearsed that conversation as a kind of joke. By 2.00 a.m. I was exhausted and looking for someone to take me home. Ma was nowhere to be found and Nhlanhla wanted me to spend the night at her parents' house with her and her bridesmaids.

'Stay, Rubi. Sim and I will bring your stuff in the morning,' Pierre suggested, his speech laboured. Sim was amused and sleepy.

So I stayed and listened to Nhlanhla's friends congratulate her on her marriage well into the morning.

At some point I walked like a zombie to find a room where I could close my eyes, eventually collapsing on the bed next to Gogo. The house was overflowing with people walking in and out, asking for dishes, bringing in the ready-cooked meat. The young girls were washing dishes and sneaking alcohol into the house. The music and conversations were loud and everyone's clothes smelled like the fire where more meat was being cooked. The atmosphere reminded me of when Baba came back from *ukuthwasa*. He was different, no more fire in his legs, and wearing strange clothes. Gogo organised *mokete* to celebrate the successful completion of his training. Many people came to our small house. I fell asleep to the sound of the drums that Baba would one day tell me about in his stories.

Cedrick's family and friends were still celebrating. They'd moved on to single-malt whiskey. The sound of their laughter and talking outside the window of the room where Gogo and I were resting finally ushered me into sleep.

My dreams take me to Cape Town; inside Afreek, headed for Pierre's office. I open the door and he is standing there with Natalie. I have been naked with the man; I have seen every emotion live on his face. One expression I am very familiar with is lust. That's what I'm seeing on his face now. Stolen, secretive lust; lust of a different colour but still the same creature. This lust colour suits his face better, looks like it is more fun. Natalie smiles and pulls her face up close to his while he whispers to her.

From shock to total heartbreak in an instant. I stand there at Pierre's office door and wait for one of them to look up; something makes Pierre lift his head. Shock and guilt erase his lighter more playful demeanour. 'Rubi ...' My name follows me as I walk away slowly. Not running like the girls do in the romantic comedies. I don't see how anyone can run when emotion suddenly pushes down on your chest like the fat bully in school who sits on you to prove a point. I get the point: I am small and these emotions are larger than me. Much larger.

Pierre is saying something else but my heart is shouting too loudly for me to hear. My feet start taking smaller steps; I'm suddenly much smaller ... younger, and my little feet are barefoot. 'Just keep walking, keep walking, don't slow down, and don't act like you're upset. Ntatemoholo will find you soon. Where is home? Rubi, don't be scared, neh? Ntatemoholo is waiting ...'

By the time I get home Ntatemoholo is not there. 'Oh no! I have to wait outside. What if ... Ntatemoholo! I'm hungry! I'm cold and I'm hurt. Okay. Mama is away at a wedding. How long is a weekend anyway? How long was that night time? Is she back already? Did they all go away without me? STOP crying, Marubini, you're already in enough trouble. Oh no! I knew I shouldn't have followed the school kids. But school sounded like so much fun. The bell always goes *ki-ting ki-ting ki-ting* and then all I hear is laughing children. I just wanted to know what was happening at school. Oh no, Ntatemoholo will think I don't love him, but school seems so nice and they all go to school and leave me behind. They all know things, and I only know how to play *morabaraba* and the names of animals on Mama's plastic table cloth in the kitchen.'

'Marubini.'

'Ntatemoholo!' I get up from the stoep where I have been sitting forever. The stoep of my childhood home was getting cold, and so was I. My Ntatemoholo's eyes move from top to bottom to make sure I am still his only granddaughter. He looks like he doesn't recognise me. I look to where his eyes seem stuck. Uh-oh, I messed! He picks me up and starts crying. 'Let's go get you bathed, okay? It's okay; you were scared, that's all.'

'Ntatemoholo, I'm sorry ... I love you, but the school ...'

'It's okay, I thought I'd lost you.'

'I'm not lost, I'm right here,' I scream, kissing my mother's father on the cheek. He's busy boiling a pot of water on the stove; he doesn't look like he believes me, though.

'Rubi, my baby, we have to wash you.'

Ntatemoholo doesn't look very happy. The frown on his face looks like he's in pain. My grandfather takes my dress off and we both realise that I don't have any underwear on. I look at my dress and the blood on it makes me cry. My grandfather takes the dress away where I can't see it; what we cannot see cannot hurt us.

'Sing the song, okay ...' he tells me, as he walks away to the kitchen. He means our bath-time song: '*Hlapa … Hlapa*. Mama is coming home soon. She doesn't need to know how dirty we got today. Playing and learning so we can grow and be clever …'

'Sing it louder, Marubini,' he shouts from the kitchen, his voice trembling with the need to let go of control so that his soul can throw up all his anger in bitter sobs. It isn't just his emotional heart that is breaking. The hurt is too much and it's hardening in his physical heart too. My grandfather is sobbing as if he'll never stop and I am covering up his sobs with the bath-time song we made up together.

After my bath, he disposes of my soiled dress. My grandfather lies down on his bed and clutches at his chest. The air going in and out of his chest slows, while I sit on the floor with my crayons, forgetting and filling in the black and white pictures with my own colours.

I wake up and Gogo is standing at the door looking at me. 'I came to wake you up. There will be a long line for the bathrooms.' It's still dark outside. 'Four o' clock,' she answers, before I ask.

'Aaaa Gogo, I just slept two hours ago.'

'You can sleep when you're on the plane back to Cape Town.' Gogo is looking at me with worry. 'What were you dreaming of?'

'Pierre …' We both laugh awkwardly and she disappears. I allow myself to cry quietly. My dreams have left me confused and heartbroken.

After a lot of morning preparation and much shouting from Nhlanhla, we finally make our way to the church for the White Wedding ceremony. Cedrick looks even older by daylight than he did the night before. Gogo is laughing at the shiny gold suit that he is wearing. '*Uyabona ke* Marubini, *imali* cannot buy you style.' Ma gives Gogo a cross look and shakes her head disapprovingly.

Throughout the long ceremony I keep glancing at Pierre. What did that dream mean? I didn't really walk in on Pierre having an intimate moment with Natalie; does that mean it never happened? And what about Ntatemoholo? Was that also just a dream or something that really happened? I have no memory of him being sick. It was a long time ago, that's probably why I don't remember. Whenever I asked Ma about it she would just tell me that Ntatemoholo had a bad heart and got sick gradually.

'Ma, these flowers are beautiful,' Simphiwe exclaims as we walk into the venue where the reception is being held. The reception is another display of Cedrick's wealth and Nhlanhla's love of all things loud. The colour scheme is white and gold. Ma's flower arrangement of white and yellow roses is the best part of the decorations.

There's expensive French Champagne that was flown into South Africa for the wedding. Pierre and Ma seem to be enjoying it. Gogo, however, says the bubbles in the drink make it difficult to enjoy. So we're having gin and tonic instead. Simphiwe laughs at Gogo for swopping one drink with bubbles for another. After a few drinks I start to feel a little more relaxed. The gin and tonic tastes too bitter for my liking but the dreams of last night feel more like a distant memory.

Cedrick's business partner is busy making a speech when the air around me grows thin. I walk outside. My heart is beating fast for no reason and the familiar nausea is creeping up on me.

'Are you okay, *cherie*?'

I didn't realise Pierre had followed me out. He looks amazing in the black suit that I picked out for him. It looks like he hasn't even sat down in it; not a crease in sight. I check my dress for stains; none. Well done, Rubi.

'Wow, you haven't called me that in a while.' I flash him a smile but it disappears too quickly. 'Can I ask you something?'

'Sure.' We can still hear Cedrick's friend talking, but his voice is distorting. He sounds like a drunk, laughing giant. There is no easy way to ask what I want to know. 'Do you have feelings for Natalie?' Pierre's face tells me he is unsure what's going on. 'Has anything ever happened between the two of you?'

'Where is this coming from?' He looks hurt, not angry like in the dream.

'I don't know ... I just want to know.'

Pierre sighs and shakes his head. 'Why don't you trust me, Rubi?' His voice sounds soft and injured.

'I never said that, Pierre. I just want to know.' I am raising my voice and he raises his eyebrows.

'No, I don't have feelings for Natalie. You're the person that I love ...'

'Nothing has ever happened between you at Afreek?'

'What are you talking about ...?' His voice tails off, his eyes searching my face. 'Are you okay, Rubi?' His hand touches my cheek and I realise that I'm crying. 'What's going on with you? And don't tell me it's about Natalie.' Now he sounds angry.

Words fly out of my mouth and I start sobbing. 'I think I killed my grandfather!'

Marubini, o a hlanya, you didn't kill Ntatemoholo *wa hao*. What's going on with you?' Ma yells at me. Her voice is angry but her face looks scared.

The celebrations at the wedding reception lasted until the early hours once again. When I woke up towards noon, the last thing on my mind was asking Ma whether I had killed her father. She, Gogo and I are having tea in the kitchen at home. Gogo asks what's wrong with me. 'I've had a feeling for a long time that you're not okay.'

Ma quickly responds: 'It's probably that epilepsy thing.'

Gogo takes a sip of her tea and ignores Ma. 'Why don't you tell us what's bothering you, *nana*?'

I look at my mother. She stares at her tea.

'Ma, why can't I remember what happened to Ntatemoholo?'

Her eyes widen at my question but her voice remains calm. 'Because it was a long time ago.'

I shake my head, knowing she isn't telling me the truth. 'Did I kill Ntatemoholo?' My voice quivers as I say it. That's when Ma has her outburst.

Gogo stirs her tea and shakes her head. 'Makosha ...'

'No Mam'Thoko!' It wasn't only Ma's voice that was afraid; her face was in on it too.

'We've tried your way. Now let's try the truth,' Gogo says calmly. 'Do you want what we did to drive this child to madness?'

Ma stands up from the table and reheats her still-warm tea in the microwave.

Gogo continues: 'You know that she doesn't have this epilepsy. She is yearning for the truth that we took away from her.'

'Ma,' my voice is begging, 'please, tell me what's happening. What truth is she talking about? And why would you rather accept that I am sick and tried to kill myself?'

She sits down again, her face angry. 'The alternative is worse. I promised Jabulani ...' Saying Baba's weakens her anger.

Simphiwe walks into the kitchen. '*San'bonani*,' he greets us, and puts a piece of paper down in front of me. Gogo looks at it and gasps, her hand covering her mouth.

It's not difficult to recognise a sketch of yourself if it's well done. Simphiwe's talent is undeniable ... and unsettling. Gogo and I are in her hut. Her hand is stretched out as she kneels next to me, smearing something on my forehead. My grandmother's other hand is holding a sharp knife that is pointed at me. My eyes are closed and I am lying on my back, with a small piece of cloth covering me. I look calm. Maybe I don't know that there's a knife pointing at me. Perhaps the me in the sketch knows that Gogo would never hurt me.

Ma slams her fist on the table. 'No! Please Mam'Thoko, don't do this.'

'It has been decided for us,' Gogo says to Ma, but her eyes are fixed on Simphiwe. For a while nobody in the kitchen says anything.

'Why are you looking at me like that, Gogo?' Simphiwe finally asks.

Gogo ignores his question. 'How long have you been doing this?'

He shrugs. 'A few weeks or months, I don't know. Gogo, what are you going to do to Rubi?'

Again Gogo doesn't answer him. She stands up from the table and disappears into one of the bedrooms to collect her things. When she returns she says, 'Don't let too much time pass, we have lots of work to do.'

Nobody moves or utters a word. My legs are tingling and my mouth tastes like tea and bile. Why is everyone being so cryptic? I glance back at Simphiwe's drawing of me and Gogo. What is happening?

We are still sitting there in silence when Pierre walks into the kitchen. Ma stands up and goes to her bedroom.

'I'm gonna go weed or something ...' Simphiwe mutters and leaves too.

I answer Pierre's question before he asks it. 'I really have no idea what's going on. But something is, and I can't leave without finding out what.'

Gogo's hut has always been cold because it was built in a shady part of her backyard. I am shivering because I am naked and the cloth she has draped me with barely covers my thighs and sits just below my shoulders.

'*Vala amehlo.*' I close my eyes as Gogo has requested. 'Don't be scared, Marubini. I'm right here. No matter what happens, I am here.' She is burning *impepho* and something else that my senses seem to recognise. I hear her breathing get deeper as she starts to meditate and connect with the ancestors. Baba did this often. Then he would make what I call 'the meditating noise' that lives in the back of the throat. Even though Ma didn't want Gogo to perform this ceremony on me, she came along with us. She still hasn't told me what this is about, saying only that if I want to do this then I should.

Ma and Simphiwe wait in Gogo's house while Gogo continues with her mysterious rituals, putting something cold on my forehead. Simphiwe's sketch jumps into my mind, stirring up ripples of fear and doubt.

Gogo puts her hand on my shin, 'Ssssshhhhhh.'

I calm down again. There is smoke filling the room, I can't see it but I can feel it. It slips into my nostrils and from there into my entire body. Gogo's glottal meditating is rocking me into a peaceful space. It is a place that seems familiar, like a house that I left many years ago. Nobody has changed a single thing about this house. All the rooms look the same. I have left pieces of myself in parts of the house. They are suspicious of me: 'Where have you been? Why did you go?' Why would I need to separate myself from myself? Who are those people outside the house? This house is the one I grew up in. It is an old house in a time that has passed. I am watching myself, but I don't remember this day.

Ntatemoholo is standing at the fence talking to the neighbour, Ntate Hlaswa. It's a warm morning and the front and back doors are open. Ma must have bathed me before leaving for work because I've already got that Vaseline glow. Ntatemoholo has a spade in his hand, which means he's going to do some work in Ma's garden.

The neighbour is talking about something I don't understand. 'It's not safe to go to work some days. How do they expect us to feed our families?'

Ntatemoholo is shaking his head. 'I heard about the violence in the townships and I thought it would be over after all those school kids died.'

'How could it be over? Children did what we could not and now we are being punished for the bloodshed!'

'Punished by who?' Ntatemoholo asks Ntate Hlaswa.

I sit on the stoep and let my skin soak the sun in. After discussing dead school children, stay-aways and no money, Ntate Hlaswa goes inside his house and Ntatemoholo continues tending to the garden.

'When can I go to school, Ntatemoholo?'

He laughs. 'When you're ready.'

I shrug in protest. 'But the other children go to school every day. Can't I go just once?' He's not even listening to me. I occupy myself with stones and ants on the stoep until Ntatemoholo tells me that it's time for lunch.

'But our story is not on yet,' I say.

'*Ja*, but I'm hungry now,' is my grandfather's response. We go inside the house and have what's left of last night's pap and morogo. 'Ma will be cross that we're eating pap for lunch,' I say. Ma didn't want Ntatemoholo and I eating pap all day. She always made suggestions like cabbage with some boiled chicken or eggs and bread.

Ntatemoholo laughs. 'Makosha is not coming back today; she's going to a friend's wedding.' Ma's friend was getting married in Katlehong. They were all going to go there after work and she would only return on Sunday. Ntatemoholo and I were on our own for the entire weekend.

'So, it's our little secret, okay?' His eyes smile at me. I nod my head and eat my warm leftovers. After lunch Ntatemoholo switches on the radio, because it's almost time for our radio story. We both know this because we heard the school bell ringing, indicating that it is lunch time. Some of the neighbourhood children are coming home for lunch. We're barely ten minutes into the story when one of Ntatemoholo's friends appears at the door. I can't remember his name but I say hello politely.

'Looks like nothing is going according to plan today,' my grandfather says. He switches the radio off and makes tea for his friend.

No story for us, so I take a doll and play in the sitting room from where I can watch the school kids. The thought enters my mind quickly. Ntatemoholo is talking to his friend and there is no afternoon radio story. The children are running back to the school. I'll just follow them and see what happens when they get to school. The big kids are running, but I don't run. I just walk slowly, with my doll swinging by my side. Nobody notices me, because most people are at work and those who aren't are having lunch inside their houses.

I can hear children singing on the playground: *'Bana ba sekolo. Bana ba sekolo …'* I know that song. Sometimes Ntatemoholo and I sing it. It's a hot day and I am walking as fast as I can, but not fast enough because when I get to the gate it's locked. Four girls are running towards the school quad, where all the children are lining up. I've missed it; now I'll never be able to go into the school. I turn around to go home but there is a stone in my shoe. The old lady who sells food outside the school is taking her empty pots into her house. Ntatemoholo and I have bought sweets from her before. Some school children don't go home for lunch. Instead they buy *kota, magwinya* with white liver paste, or whatever she spent all morning cooking. She lives just across the road from the school, so she's taking her pots back into her house. While I'm trying to shake the stone out of my sandal, I see the old woman appear at her window.

'Hey, *mtana ka Jabu!*' She knows my father; I smile and wave. *'Ufunani lapho?'* She wants to know why I'm standing outside the school gates. I don't respond and she tells me, very sternly, to go home. A young man walks into her yard. She doesn't acknowledge him, her eyes still fixed on me. *'Hamb' ekhaya manje!'*

The young man calls from her front door, *'Ko ko*, do you still have chicken feet left, *magriza?'* I hear her answer, sounding cross: 'I'm not your *magriza, wena mfana.'*

I finally manage to kick the stone out of my shoe. But before I can take even one step towards home, I feel my feet leaving the ground. A big hand is covering my mouth and I'm being carried into the school yard. My doll falls to the ground as I kick and struggle and try to wriggle myself free from the cold hands that are holding me. The school gate is locked again, my doll lying outside. I'm now in a cold room in the school grounds. In the corner of the room stands the monster who knows the corners of my sitting room in Cape Town. I recognise his presence. The walls of this house must be made of ice, because I can't stop shivering.

I close my eyes and open them again. Now I'm in Baba's hut and it's night time. He is mixing something in a bowl. 'Don't be scared, uBaba is going to fix this.' I'm sitting on the floor in my pyjamas, with my legs crossed. My father grabs an old soft-drink bottle filled with a light-brown liquid. He pours it into the bowl and keeps stirring the mixture. 'Drink this.' It smells terrible.

'No.' I fold my arms and look away.

'It's good for you ...'

I unfold my arms and look at Baba suspiciously.

'It's like the one from last night, I know it is.'

He frowns and mumbles something about needing to make it stronger.

'What do you remember from last night, Marubini?'

I point at the bowl in his hands. 'You made me drink that and I slept. I don't like it, Baba.'

He is putting some dried herbs into the mixture and he isn't looking at me. 'You have to do this for me, Marubini.'

I take the bowl from his hands and hold my nose as I drink the mixture. Immediately I start to feel sleepy. My father's arms catch me as my whole body becomes a collapsed lump of skin and bones. The bowl rolls away from us and I watch it from behind sightless eyes. Then I focus my attention on Baba holding me in his arms. I am there with my father, but I am also standing by the hut door. Baba lays me down on the cow skin in the middle of the room and sits cross-legged with his back to me.

'I know you're there. Come closer,' he invites me. I walk out of the shadows and stand in front of my father. 'I hate to do this to you but I have to. You understand this but ...' he sighs and points at my little body lying on the ground, '... she doesn't. I know you cannot speak back to me, Marubini. But I need you to listen to me.'

I am not sure if my father can see me. I'm not even sure if I am something that can be seen, but I know he senses me.

'My teacher once told me a story about a healer who was able to remove something painful from someone he loved. Nobody wants to see someone they love suffer. I was not able to protect you, but I won't let you suffer forever. What kind of healer would I be?'

I want to ask Baba a question but I don't know where my voice has gone to.

'uGogo wakho says that's just a story, but I have to try to put things right. How else will I be able to look your mother in the face? How will I live with myself?'

Baba takes a razor blade and starts making small incisions on my left wrist and the back of my neck. He puts small bowls beneath my wrist and neck; blood starts dripping into the bowls. He takes what looks like a big, dry, grey bush and breaks off branches that he puts around me. The branches start burning and Baba closes his eyes and begins chanting words that seem familiar to me. My blood is collecting slowly in the bowls. I notice that my blood is red when it leaves my skin, but it becomes black as it collects in the bowls.

There is blood on the bed and on my legs. The monster gets off me and groans. I'm crying quietly because I don't want him to hit me again. I fear him more than I do the pain that is burning into me. Outside the sun has set and the school looks like an eerie, desolate forest. The trees are scary giants, making sure that I don't run away. My wrists smell like mildew where his hands held me down. The pain is unbearable and I just want to go home. I breathe out and I can see the hot air leaving my body, but the pain between my legs remains. The monster is standing at the window watching something.

There are voices outside; the people are calling out a name and it sounds like 'Banzi'. 'Banzi, *bula* gate! There is a child missing.' The voices are getting louder. 'Have you seen a small child here?'

'Of course he has seen her. He knows all the children in this neighbourhood. We found her doll right here outside the gate.'

The monster turns towards me and for the first time I see his face. He's not a monster at all. He's Banzi, the school groundskeeper. All the school children know him. My grandfather knows him. I have seen him several times while walking with Ma in the streets of our neighbourhood. He lives in the school grounds and makes a jingling sound when he walks. There are many keys on his belt loop and they jingle when he moves. It's those same keys that caused welts on my thighs when he was on top of me a few minutes ago. My head hurts and my eyes are swollen from crying. Banzi looks at me and the look scares me even more.

He grabs my arm and drags me off the bed. 'Stay,' he barks. The bark is human. It belongs not to a monster but to a grown-up, one that I know. I back up under the table where his two-plate stove and dishes are resting. He opens the door and calls, 'What is all this shouting about?'

I hear my grandfather's voice. 'My grandchild is missing. Have you seen her?'

More voices start shouting, 'Have you seen the child, Banzi? Where is she? We know you know where she is. Who else could have taken a child here?'

Someone says, 'We don't know that it's him. Banzi, just let us into the house to check for ourselves if she's here.'

He growls at them. That one is an animal growl and it makes me cover my head with my arms. He growled at me like that when I screamed and ran for the door. I had not expected he would hit me so hard across the face. I don't know how long he hit me for; I just know that I don't want it to happen again.

'No.' As soon as he says that there is a roar from the angry mob. '*Kulungile*. I will allow that *magriza* to come and have a look, but nobody else. This is my house and you people are accusing me of something serious.'

He walks outside with the jingling sound following him. I see a shadow by the door and then a person pokes her head around the door. It's the old woman from across the road. I am too terrified to move, but I hope she can see the hot air leaving my body and rising above the table that I'm hiding under. I think she can see me. But then she turns her attention to the other side of the room where the bloody bed is. She gasps, and then I don't see her again.

All the terror from under the table is leaving my body in a few drops of blood. The memories drip into the bowl beneath my neck and pool in the sticky black blood. This is not right, I don't feel right and I'm concerned. I want to tell Baba that we cannot keep draining me of my memories and pain like this. He has his back to me while he meditates next to my body. It looks so small and frail lying there. I can see outside the little window of the hut. My mother is sitting on the stoep looking at the door that stands between her and my body lying on the floor. 'It's so wrong, Mama, tell Baba to stop now. It's been too many nights. My body is tired. I'm always confused.' But my essence has no voice and she cannot sense me. Only Baba can.

'She will recover from this, stop worrying. The body's mind is confused but it will pass. She will be better, you'll see.' Baba is speaking to me, I think, in his deep, glottal, meditating voice. His eyes are closed. He doesn't see what I see.

There are a few platinum drops falling into the bowl. Falling from my neck into the sticky black blood. My eyes notice another strange drop from my wrist. That one is gold. This doesn't feel right. Baba doesn't sense my despair because he's too deep in his meditation. I wish Mama could hear me. But her eyes are stuck behind the closed door and I am nothing but an essence. I summon all my will: 'Ma, please!'

She stands up suddenly and comes to sit by the door. 'Jabulani, I know you think you're doing the right thing but what if we're hurting her?' She knows Baba can't hear her when he's in this state, and if he can he chooses not to listen.

'You know how many babies we lost before Marubini came. I don't want to lose her ... Think how you will feel if something goes wrong.' Her voice is cracking. 'Jabu. Please, s'thandwa sam', just give me back my baby, please.' My mother is crying and I can't stand it. 'Talk to me

Jabulani, I know you can hear me!' She bangs her fist on the door but Baba seems unmoved. The black, gold and platinum drops continue to leave my body. Nobody but me can see them. Nobody but me can see that there is something good being torn away with the bad.

My mouth has no moisture in it. I've got used to the pain that has moved into my body. Banzi left in the morning. Before he left, he made me pap and eggs for breakfast. When I vomited he got very angry and punched me in the face.

'I'm sorry. I don't want to hurt you. You know that, Marubini.' He only ever spoke to me after he'd hurt me. The rest of the time he just stared at me. 'I just get angry if you don't eat. How else will you grow?'

I'm crying quietly, sitting on the floor near the table where I had hidden the night before. The blood on the sheets has my full attention. Banzi sees this and pulls the sheets off the bed. 'It's okay. You'll feel better soon.'

I wasn't sure where the most pain was coming from anymore. With my legs stretched out on the floor, the cold cement numbs some of my pain. My throat is still sore from what happened the night before. After all the people had left, Banzi looked very upset. 'Did you say anything?' There was spit flying out of his mouth. I shook my head and made myself smaller under the table. A whimper came out of my mouth: 'I want to go home.' That made him even more furious. 'You're not going anywhere!' He walked out of the house with the big zinc tub. His breathing was heavy as he walked back in and threw the full tub down on the floor. Water splashed all over. I tried to kick his hands away when he reached for me. He grabbed me by the leg and kicked the door shut. I wasn't expecting him to hold my head beneath the cold water for so long. Water entered my lungs and I wriggled furiously. He pulled my head up and whispered in my ear, 'I will kill you if you try to leave me. Don't you see how much I love you?' I don't know how many times he held my head under the water. I just remember opening my eyes and finding him on top of me again. A small scream escaped from my burning throat and then my eyes slammed shut.

Now I am alone. I don't know what to do. The door is locked. I heard the jingling of the keys and the snap the lock made after Banzi walked out. I drift in and out of sleep and change position when the pain gets too much on one side or the other. A loud crack jolts me out of sleep. I cover my mouth to stop my scream from escaping. Another loud crack and the door flies open. I crawl back under the table.

'Marubini.' It's not Banzi. What if it's another person who wants to hurt me? I see feet moving around the room and then a face appears under the table. It's the old woman who was here last night. She reaches for me and I wince. 'There you are – thank goodness! I thought you were dead.' Her face squeezes tears from her old eyes. I grab her hand and she picks me up.

The school gate is still locked. We escape through a hole in the fence. The old lady puts me down on the ground and whispers in my ear, 'Run home, child. Run!' As soon as my feet hit the ground, I start to hobble home. I'm wearing only one shoe but I don't even notice. Ntatemoholo is waiting for me. He will think I don't love him anymore. The streets are empty and there's nobody home in the houses. What if they all moved away and left me because I let Banzi take me?

The lines in the colouring book are blurring. There is a dripping sound coming from underneath the table. It's coming from me, the chair I'm sitting on. My panties are soaked. I must have had another accident. The doors are locked, I heard Ntatemoholo do it while I was putting my socks on. My socks are itchy now because they are wet. A key is turning in the door; afraid, I hide under the table. What if Banzi has keys to all our houses? He knows that I'm not there, in his room where he told me to stay, and he knows where I live.

'Ntatemoholo!' My voice is shrill and high-pitched. I don't even recognise it. The person approaching me has no jingling music accompanying them. The edge of the table cloth rises like the curtain of a puppet show. It's my mother! Her eyes are huge with surprise and she is reaching out for me. I'm wild with fear and my struggling body has a mind of its own.

'Marubini, what's wrong with you?' She sounds scared. Ntatemoholo's feet drag him into the room and Ma immediately asks, 'What is wrong with Marubini?'

Ntatemoholo calls my name. I know he cannot bend down to look at me. His old bones won't allow it. He bangs his hand on the table above me. 'Marubini.' I don't know how many times he says my name, but eventually I stop screaming.

Two pairs of feet walk out of the house. A few minutes later my mother screams. Everything after that is screams: waking up to my own screams; the screams of the principal who first discovered Banzi's charred arm trying to break through the window of his burned room; Ntatemoholo screaming at Ma, 'How could you do that, Makosha?'; Ma screaming when Ntatemoholo collapsed; the screams in my dreams. Then came the crying.

Baba came home and took turns holding his wife until she slept then getting up to hold his crying daughter. He did his crying when he was alone. Ntatemoholo died and the tears wouldn't leave us alone.

Whenever we thought we were a river, they showed us the ocean from which they flowed.

An old lady walked into our house one day. She also came to cry. Ma let her talk and cry. Words leave her mouth and run past me as I play with my puzzles in my room.

'I should have come to you long ago. My shame kept me from doing it. When I was a young woman, I fell in love with a young man. I fell in love and somehow I stayed where I had fallen. I was never above love or beside him, just where I had fallen; grateful for whatever scraps of love I got. At the bottom where I lay, I began to see shadows. But we had just had a baby and I didn't want to ruin things. It was my purse that showed me the horror of my silence. One day like any other day, I went out to the store for mealie meal. My purse called me back. I had forgotten it on the kitchen table. I can never forget what I saw when I walked in. There, next to the purse, lay my baby, crying and screeching while her father did unthinkable things to her. My infant died that night because the man I chose ripped her in two. His family kicked me out of our house. It was my child that he had killed and yet I was called a liar, a witch, and cast aside.

'When I moved here I knew exactly who that man at the school was. I recognised the darkness in him, which is why I started selling food to the school children and keeping an eye on them. I am not the only person who suspected that this man was a monster. Why else would all of us head straight to his room on the school grounds when a child went missing? Why did none of us speak up with our suspicions? But we had no proof of anything.

'That night when he let me into his room, I saw the blood on his bed. I knew she had been there but I thought he had killed her. I was too distraught to say anything. The thought of another child suffering the same terrible fate right under my nose was too much for me ...

'All that night I had dreams about my child. What if I had carried her on my back to the shop with me that day? Would she be alive now? Or did I always know that my husband was going to kill her?

'The next day, I watched from my window until I saw Banzi leave. Then I took my axe and broke down the door of his room. It was my child that I was looking for. But it was yours that I found there. For many nights after that I wandered the streets of darkness. It was on one of those nights that I saw you bolt Banzi's door from the outside. You don't know this, Mama, but I stood and watched that beautiful, merciless fire with you. Your fire did what I could not do.'

Baba is talking to me again; even though I am not in my body, he can sense where I am in the room.

'I had only ever heard bits and pieces of the healer's story,' he tells me. 'Gogo finally told me the rest of it. "I thought this was all I had to do to make you well again. But I was wrong." She found out the rest from another old healer who was one of the first people to hear the story,' He looks sad.

'That man who tried to take away something painful ... He became the owner of the hurt. He drained it out, so it became his duty to guard it and never let it spread further. The pain was now his burden.

'The healer in the story that my teacher told me, his wife had gone through something painful while he was away gathering herbs and medicine. A bad man like Banzi hurt her and when the healer came back his wife wasn't the same. She just sat and cried all day and that broke his heart. Every healer knows that memories are located in the body. It is the blood that keeps them in the body. So one day he gave his wife something that would make her sleep and he started draining the bad memories from her body. The story says that he made incisions in the back of her neck, because it was something in the past that he was trying to remove. He also cut her left wrist, because she was right-handed and the darkness always attacks us where we are weak. I thought that was all I had to do for you. Drain out the pain until the blood stopped turning black in the bowl. But now I know that's not enough.'

I can feel his sadness as he says it. 'Gogo has been asking all the old healers she knows about this story. One old woman told her that I would have to leave in order for you to get better. I'm the person who drained the pain and darkness out of you, and I now own it. As long as I am near you, the darkness will try to get back into you. The healer who first did this also had to leave his wife. He knew from the beginning that he would have to go as far away from her as possible, but he did it anyway.'

Baba has my small hand in his and he is crying. My presence feels heavy. 'I would rather leave you happy than live knowing that I did nothing to heal your pain. The old woman told your Gogo that I have to bury this darkness in the place where we first lived ...' Baba cannot talk anymore. He cries and squeezes my hand. 'I have to go back to the place where we *abantu* were once kings, queens and wise scholars of the stars and moons. That's where I have to bury your darkness if we're ever going to be together. I'm going to walk to the source of *abantu* and let our beginnings take this burden from me. That is where the strongest ancestors are. Only they can take this burden from me.' I don't understand what Baba is saying. I don't want him to go away. 'Never be afraid, Marubini, because *ubaba uyak'thanda*, and I will never let anyone hurt you again.'

'Mam'Thoko, she is waking up.' Ma and Gogo's faces appear in front of me. I'm in my bed in Soweto.

'She must have known that I came to see her.' That is Nkgono's voice approaching. She is walking slowly, relying on her stick to help her along.

Ma eases me back onto the bed. 'No, don't try to get up.'

Simphiwe and Pierre show their faces at the door. I'm so relieved to see them. I am not certain how I'm feeling or what has happened to me.

Gogo answers my question before I ask it. 'A few days. You were mumbling and screaming like a mad woman.'

Ma squeezes my hand. The room quickly becomes crowded with people I love. They are all looking at me expectantly. I don't know what to say to them. I'm crying, and I don't know why. They gather around me and ask me how I feel. 'Sore.' I mean that physically and emotionally. My hand strokes the place where my father made incisions on my left wrist.

'You must have been so desperate to remember,' Gogo says. She is not looking me in the eye, not even really talking to me. From the expressions on the faces around me, I know that there are no secrets between us anymore.

Ma waves people out of the room. 'Out, out, out. Can't you see that she is tired?'

My tongue is sticking to the roof of my mouth. Ma sees me eyeing the jug of water next to me. 'You must be dying of thirst.' She helps me sit up and slots pillows between me and the wall. 'I suppose you have questions.' Ma looks and sounds different to me. How could I have been blind to who she truly is?

'Were you afraid?' I ask her. She knows what I'm talking about.

'No. I was too angry to be afraid. I hated seeing you so changed, always so scared.' I want to ask about the other babies she lost, but how do I explain how I know about them? It feels like I've only just met Ma and I don't want to offend her with too many questions.

'Are you sorry you did it?'

She narrows her eyes and relaxes her clenched hands. 'No.'

I enjoy my mother's huge presence and the silence between us. Inside of me, there is a lot going on. My mind is shuffling memories into places that had become arid.

'Pierre called every day and eventually came to see you for himself ...' Ma laughs at me rolling my eyes. 'You are so hard on everyone, Marubini. Don't be so afraid to let people all the way in. That man loves you. I can see he does.'

'I think I know it too. I've just always felt like something was missing. Like sometimes I don't know what I'm supposed to feel or ...'

Ma sighs. 'I should never have let Jabulani do what he did, but he was afraid of what the constant fear and pain would eventually do to you.'

'It's okay, Mama. I know you did it to protect me.' I remember Baba saying that he had to go away to the source, to the strongest ancestors. Ma doesn't know about his plans to deliver the pain he acquired from me to where we *abantu* come from. She doesn't need to know that her husband intended to leave her to go and rid himself of *my* pain. He didn't even say where that place was.

'You look tired, *nana*, get some sleep.'

'But Ma, I'm so hungry.'

Ma laughs at that and calls Simphiwe. He appears at the door. 'Ma?'

'Your sister is hungry; please get her something to eat.'

A smile spreads across his face, 'She's always hungry.' Then he slips away before Ma can scold him.

Ma gives me time to talk to Pierre while I have my lunch. There is so much I want to tell him.

'How are you feeling?'

'Honestly ... I don't know. I feel like I have been living as half of myself all this time.'

'It's okay to feel like that. You're probably still processing it all.' Pierre sits on the bed next to me and holds my hand. I look at our reflections in the mirror. There are dark rings under my eyes, my lips are dry and the brown of my skin is dull. Pierre caresses my arm and my skin illuminates beneath his hand. I close my eyes and allow myself just to feel. His concern and love seeps into me and I fall asleep.

Unathi's Malaika is telling Gogo the story of Jack and the 'Beemstock'. She is looking up at my grandmother, tilting her head with every twist in the story and nodding when the story gets exciting. Nkgono likes this story; she is eating her nuts and laughing at how impossible it all sounds. Gogo, however, stares blankly at Malaika. She turns to Unathi and says, 'This is a very violent story. Why is this little boy Jack involved in a home invasion?' Nkgono shakes her head and carries on shelling her peanuts.

'It's just a story, Gogo,' I say from where I'm sitting.

'A story about going into people's homes and stealing? *Cha!*' My Gogo shakes her head and claps her hands. Malaika is not in any way deterred; she just carries on telling her story more loudly.

I'm still having nightmares and I can't seem to make sense of any of them. Sometimes Simphiwe will have drawn something that has happened in my dreams. Some afternoons he won't want to talk to anyone and just sits in the sitting room, staring woefully out the window. When I ask him what's wrong, he says there is something stewing and he just has to sit and wait till it's done.

Nkgono doesn't entertain his moods. When he said that, she nudged me and said: 'Sounds like the onset of diarrhoea.'

Gogo says we should be sensitive to Simphiwe's moods; he's going through something that he cannot yet control. Most of the drawings are of me as a child. I don't like to look at them and Simphiwe doesn't like to show them to people. He says it feels like people are staring at his insides. My nightmares seem to be affecting Ma badly. Every time I scream myself awake she is there looking at me, completely horrified.

'Tell me what to do for you. I don't want to hear my child scream like this.' I heard her telling Nkgono that she cannot bear to live through this nightmare again. Nkgono didn't say anything; she just let her daughter cry.

Unathi decided that she would brave seeing her family in Soweto for the holidays, just so she could see me.

'How's your mother?' I ask her.

'The same ... We are never going to see eye to eye, I guess. William and I have made our peace with it. He is going to spend Christmas with his family in Malawi ...' Unathi rests her head on her hand and kicks her shoes off. 'I'm thinking of going with him. I don't want to be without him. How are you?' she asks, full of concern.

I am unsure, as always, how to answer this question. My mind feels like it's buzzing with activity that I am unable to decipher.

Someone needs to give me the code. I know what has caused this disturbance but I'm not sure how to pull it all together so that it makes sense to me. I told Unathi about the man at the school who attacked me, but not about what my parents did to try and heal me. 'I guess I'm just taking it easy. I'm always so tired and my family won't let me do anything.' Not entirely true, because last night I baked with Nkgono, but I was not allowed to stand for too long.

'That's good, Ru. At least now you know what's wrong with you. So then ... you don't have the Calling like your father?'

According to Gogo, it's too soon to tell if I have the Calling or not. She is convinced the gift has passed on to Simphiwe. 'It's too early to decide anything, Marubini. These things show themselves in their own time. They need us to respect them,' Gogo keeps telling me, when I get impatient with not having answers.

One of the things I am not enjoying about being home for so long is that everyone in the neighbourhood knows I'm back. We've had visitors almost every day, who have come to check how I am, talk to Gogo and see how grown up 'little Simphiwe' is. 'Ha, the last time we saw you, you were so small.' 'Marubini, it's nice to see that you're home. How is the Cape?' 'Thokoza Gogo, how are you keeping these days?'

Among these unwelcome visitors was one of my ex-boyfriends. Ma laughed when he walked in through the kitchen door. She couldn't help embarrassing both Thabo and I.

'Hoowee, Marubini, guess who's here?' I hadn't even made it out of my room to see when she answered the question for me: 'It's my son-in-law, Thabo.' I heard Thabo laugh cheerfully; he obviously enjoyed my mother's playful name for him.

'Do you want to do this or not?' I asked Thabo. He was standing in the corner while I was busy taking my clothes off. 'Thabo, you said you wanted to do this and now *o a tshaba*.' I carry on trying to provoke him into sleeping with me. It was the first time I had ever got naked in front of a boy, but I certainly wasn't going to act like it.

'Rubi, don't you want me to kiss you first or something?' I ignored his question and got under the covers, unable to believe that Mr I-will-love-you-down was suddenly acting like a school girl. If my mother knew that her sixteen-year-old daughter was about to have sex with an eighteen-year-old boy, she would have had a heart attack. Especially since Thabo had been to the house and Ma always described him as 'lovely' and respectful. Thabo's grandmother lived in Diepkloof where my family home was, so he had already spent many holidays trying to impress my mother. His parents stayed near our school and Ma would pick me up from his house twice a week. On Mondays and Thursdays he helped me with Science and I sometimes helped him with English essays. He always told me how impressed he was with my brain.

'You're helping me with Matric work, you should be proud of yourself.'

I would tease him and say, 'And you're helping me with Grade 10 work, you should be proud that you still remember it.'

For a boy in Matric, Thabo was acting disappointingly prim, like he had never seen a girl naked. 'Thabo, you have done this before, right?' He looked away for a moment and then took his shirt off.

All of this had started as we walked together to his house after school. His parents were away for the weekend. Ma was going to pick us up from his house after work and drop Thabo off at his grandmother's house. Thabo's mom had already told Ma they were going away, so I knew that we were going to be there alone.

Thabo was in his final year of high school and he didn't act like the usual high-school idiot. Most of his friends behaved like morons, but they weren't my problem. We had been friends before we started dating and our relationship was all of eight months old by that time. The question of whether or not we would have sex had never come up; until we arrived at his house, that is.

After offering me a beverage he jumped straight into the topic: 'Rubi, we've been together for a while now.'

'I know, in some countries we would be considered married.' My joke didn't go down too well. My boyfriend looked away uncomfortably and offered me some juice. Boys were afraid of marriage; I made a mental note of that.

'Chateau-Thabo' was our last stop and he made a point of sitting on the bed, to make sure I understood that we would be spending more time there. I didn't sit down.

'*Manje*? What's wrong, Rubi?'

His parents never let us sit in his room alone. We did our homework at their dining-room table or outside by the pool.

'Nothing. I'm just not comfortable sitting in your room, that's all; why don't we go out to the pool and ...'

'No, let's talk.' There was definitely a hint of aggression there, but the look I gave him stopped it dead in its tracks.

'Why can't we talk outside?'

What Thabo said next is something that would become an inside joke between me and my friends for years. 'Because,' he said biting his lip, 'I wanna love you down.' I said nothing. He continued, 'Let me love you down, girl.'

At that moment I was sorry that young South African boys were allowed to listen to the likes of Silk and Jodeci. I didn't care that

American girls thought it was okay for men to say ridiculous things like 'freaking you is all I need', but for me it was not good enough. Who spoke like that anyway? While the 'lip-licking thing' worked for LL Cool J, I wasn't so sure about Thabo's big juicy African lips getting soaked and then him expecting me to like it. I was hesitant and he was too. Ma always said I had to be sure that it was what I wanted before I did it.

'Why?'

Thabo almost fell over. 'Why what?'

'Why now?'

'Why not now, Rubi?'

I didn't have an answer and neither did he. I sat down next to him and sighed. I felt ready, but I wanted a sign. I was waiting for some magic words from Thabo.

'What are we actually waiting for?' he asked.

I shrugged. I really didn't know what we were waiting for. I certainly wasn't waiting for Thabo to get smarter. Nkgono once told me that 'boys only get smarter when they are too old to have sex'. She thought that was really funny. I didn't even understand what it meant.

'Okay fine, but you'll have to help me with my Science project this weekend.'

'And by "help", I assume you mean do most of it,' Thabo said tiredly.

We laughed and then silence fell. There was no possibility of rejection between us at this point. Thabo had told me what he wanted and I didn't reject him. It seemed he was just happy with a 'yes'. As if all he wanted was to know that we *could* have sex. Now that he knew, he'd reverted to his old self again. I, on the other hand, wanted to get it over and done with. Surely once we had moved past the pain, I could enjoy it? My curiosity had got the better of me; Thabo's curiosity seemed appeased, but mine wasn't. So I started undressing.

Having been through 'sex education' at school and at home, I knew that I had a vagina that Thabo was going to stick his erect penis into. From my time with Nkgono I understood that it was a big step and that it would change my life forever. My grandmother also explained to me that it would be an uncomfortable and perhaps even painful experience, and that was why it was important to make sure that the person I chose to have sex with for the first time was worth all the discomfort that came before the 'exciting parts'. Nkgono sure had a way of explaining things. She said if I was able to understand that my new patent shoes caused calluses on my feet that were used to being naked and caressing the soil that covered my forefathers, until my feet got used to the shoes, then I would be 'responsible' enough to understand the concept of sharing my first time with someone worthwhile. Like many kids who grew up in rural spaces I was not afraid of my body and did not consider it something to be ashamed of.

Thabo did not have the advantage of being properly educated by people wiser than him. All his knowledge, he picked up from the 'okes' before and after rugby matches, or after drinking a couple of 'sneaked-in' beers at a friend's braai, and so on. Everything he had learned, he learned with girls who were also unsure. There was no room in his mind that contained the kind of education I had received while living with Nkgono.

I looked at him and thought Nkgono would approve of Thabo. Although I'm sure she would have said something about the size of his ears. He was always polite to teachers and parents. His gracious nature was something he revealed to me too. I found other boys crude and bullish by comparison. I approved of him, and that's all that mattered to me. I felt ready and Thabo was the person I chose.

He joined me under the covers, naked, and started kissing my neck. My nerves were killing me and I tried to relax by focusing on the table where our school bags sat, next to some of his trophies. I had no idea that he had participated in the Maths and Science Olympiads. An inexperienced over-achiever. A distinctive poking was keeping my thoughts away from bags, Science and Maths.

'Thabo ...' He looked at me hazily. 'You're poking me.'

His erect penis was not something new to me. It was a constant in our relationship. It was like a third party that didn't really need an invite. It was triggered by me whispering into his ear, the wind blowing my dress up, my lips on his neck, or even just the sight of me (that one got me every time) and other things that I would never know about.

I knew what was going to happen but I still had no idea how to do it. After much kissing, nibbling and sucking, I felt that we were ready to move forward so I said, 'Thabo, can we please just do it already?' I was anxious to get the pain part over with. Thabo fumbled around and eventually pulled out a condom from under his pillow. Cheeky bastard had the whole thing planned! I wouldn't be surprised if he had sent his parents on holiday just so he could have sex with me.

He was kneeling between my spread legs, gazing at what lay there while trying to roll the condom on. Out of curiosity I looked too; maybe something was wrong and he didn't know how to tell me. All the things he had seen in his stash of porn magazines, which I'd discovered in the back of his cupboard, had materialised. He had the look of a person who had bitten off more than he could chew. I glanced down between my legs and everything seemed in order. I even noticed that I was aroused, so why was the boy in front of me stalling?

After taking in the scene that he wasn't sure he would see again, he rolled the condom on properly and pointed his loaded weapon towards where it needed to go. I looked away and waited for something like a cut or the kind of pain you experience when you kick a wall. My pulse reverberated throughout my whole body. I was convinced Thabo could feel it too. My palms were sweaty and I was suddenly aware of my nudity, and the sounds around me. I licked my dry lips and waited. All I could feel was hardness wrapped in latex rubbing against my moisture. I let out an unsure moan because the sensation was strange and I might actually have started enjoying it. Maybe my partner wasn't so inexperienced.

Moving up, he pressed a little too hard on something and I winced.

'Sorry ...' he stopped moving and I didn't say anything. After what felt like a cloudburst between my legs, he eased his body down onto mine and pushed into me.

The pain that came next was unlike anything I'd expected and I tensed; he kept pushing. I squeezed every muscle in my body tighter. Sighing, he pushed again and forced my legs open.

'Please relax,' he begged.

Relax? Would he relax if someone was tearing away at his flesh? He stopped pushing for a moment and I relaxed a little. Seeing an opportunity to go all the way into my core he gave one last push and I gasped.

An unbelievable feeling of intrusion was overwhelming me, but I couldn't go back, I had made a decision. From the pain and weird sensations, I couldn't tell whether it was a good one or not. But I could just imagine his reaction if I suddenly wanted to stop. So I lay there and let the pain keep me interested. I tried to think of all the reasons why I should continue with this ... aside from Thabo's frustration if I said 'stop'. All my friends thought he was good looking and I found him attractive too ... Pain intruded on my thoughts again. After a few more 'reasons not to stop' I noticed that the pain was not so bad anymore and it was actually starting to feel good. I never really got the opportunity to enjoy the sensation though, because he climaxed, got off me and lay next to me with what looked like a smile and a grimace. I couldn't believe it was over so quickly. What about my pleasure? I thought to myself.

Once Thabo had recovered from his seizure of pleasure, I tapped him on the shoulder and said, 'Why are you falling asleep? What about me?'

He half opened his eyes and rolled his eyeballs. 'We can do it again when I wake up,' he said before falling asleep again. I lay there quietly while he slept and the longer I lay there the angrier I got. I was under the impression that sex was supposed to be pleasurable for both parties. At least that's how it looks in the movies. In the movies with the white people, that is. The girl is lying there with some kind of heavenly virginal light around her and the caring boy on top of her. They stare into each other's eyes while things happen by themselves below the waist. In the movies with black people it's usually more explicit. They don't show below the waist but the guy is talking dirty to the girl and she is enjoying the super-energetic deed even though she looks like she's in pain.

I didn't get the white or the black TV version. Mine was grey and uncomfortable. I was not going to leave without my pleasure, so I woke Thabo up and we had sex again. The second time around was much better than the first because I knew what to expect now, but none of the awkwardness disappeared. After that we never argued about sex again and we carried on enjoying it. I was already on the pill to 'regulate' my periods. Thabo's parents were not blind, they had made condoms readily available to their son, so we were well equipped in that regard. The more I had sex the more I enjoyed it, but I made sure never to tell my friends too much about my sex life. It was something that I shared with Thabo only. He paid me more attention when it was just the two of us and I loved that he could only share this with me. We even learned new things together. I was never scared to learn. I would insist that we do new things all the time, sometimes to Thabo's dismay. Ngono's no-holds-barred education was private, sacred and valuable.

'My ex-boyfriend from high school came to see me.' I'm smiling stupidly as I say it.

Unathi bursts into fits of giggles. 'Who? Not Thabo the rugby player?'

'Yes, that's the one. My mother was so happy to see him.' It was the first time I had seen Ma smile properly since I had emerged from Gogo's hut.

'Why did you two break up, remind me?'

'Aaargh. Some stupid high-school drama ... I think.'

'Soooo, what did he want?'

'His mother told him I was here and he came to say hello, that's all.'

There's a teenage girl inside Unathi, threatening to jump out and scream. She looks like she is going to pass out from excitement. She asks me many questions about Thabo and whether his ears are still 'ginormous'.

There were still elements of Young Thabo in the face and mannerisms of Grown-up Thabo. He was as funny as ever, but his humour seemed to be masking something. After we let the awkwardness of once being young, stupid and naked together subside, he relaxed a bit.

'I'm surprised that you are not married yet, Rubi.' Young Thabo appeared in his eyes.

'Oh please, Thabo! You know how bossy I am.'

Older Thabo returned and sighed. '*Ja*, marriage isn't everything it's made out to be anyway.' Young Thabo doesn't make an appearance while he tells the story of how he got married and it didn't work out.

'*Hau* shame, so he came to see if you are available,' Unathi says, making fun of me.

'No, *wena*!' I laugh unexpectedly.

'You haven't been yourself lately.'

Simphiwe doesn't answer immediately. He's gazing at a young girl outside the restaurant who's talking animatedly on her phone and waiting for the moment to cross the road safely. Melville is buzzing with the festive season madness that South Africans always get swept up in just before Christmas.

My brother looks back at me and shrugs. 'Sometimes I don't feel like I belong at home.' This is not news. Sim spends a lot of time at boarding school and he doesn't really have friends in our neighbourhood. Usually this doesn't bother him, but this December he seems constantly moody. His ever-busy phone has been lying around the house very neglected.

'What about Tshepo or Gavin? Why don't you go spend some time with them?'

'I don't feel like hanging out.' The waitress hovers over us and drops our drinks onto the table in front of us.

'You shouldn't be drinking, Rubi,' my little brother tells me disapprovingly.

'Oh come on, it's just one drink. Are you gonna tell Ma?'

'No, I'm gonna tell Gogo and Nkgono, they will sort you out.' A smile peeks from his lips and then disappears.

'What's really wrong, Sim? You can tell me.'

'How did Baba die, exactly?'

Ma had never made our father into a phantom. She spoke about him as if he was as real and alive as the rest of us. As a toddler, Simphiwe knew that he had a father and that his father loved him very much. The three of us had pictures of Baba in our rooms and every night before he slept Simphiwe would kiss Baba's picture and say, 'Good night, Baba.'

Speaking about our father has always been encouraged in our household. 'I want you to know that just because he is not here doesn't mean that he is not a big part of our lives,' Ma would say. The one thing she has never done is talk about how Baba died. 'The how is not important. I don't want my children to associate their father with a brutal end,' she'd say. I found out only accidentally what happened and it was not something I ever wanted to discuss, with anyone.

'Why do you ask? You know what happened. It was a politically chaotic time and ...'

'You of all people know how lies can hurt us. Please, Rubi, just tell me what really happened to Baba. I know you and Ma want to protect me but ...' His voice tails off. All his life Sim knew that his father died after being attacked on a train. The version that was told to him by Ma was that Baba was killed after being thrown off the train and his remains were never found or claimed. Such things were not unusual in those violent times when so many were intentionally killed or simply disappeared and the South African government treated dead black bodies with contempt. How many families had 'missing' as a branch of their family tree?

I know I shouldn't tell him the full story. Ma would say it's not my place. Sighing, I explain to my brother what did happen to our father, just as I heard it. As I talk, his face remains blank; no shock, sadness or disbelief on it.

'Are you okay, Sim?'

'Do you believe any of it? They said he was chased off a train and burned to death?'

His blank look is making me nervous. I nod and wait for him explain to me why he looks so unconvinced. He reaches for his back-pack and puts a few pieces of paper down on the table in front of me.

All the sketches are of the same man. In one sketch he is sitting outside a hut; there is a river flowing past his home. He's sitting on a mat and his hand is held up above his eyes, shielding them from the sun. In another sketch the man is meditating inside the hut. His hunched back is to me and all I can see is what's in front of him. On the floor is a picture of a small girl, eyes partially closed and face squeezed into a smile of ecstasy. She is holding an ice-cream cone and some of the sweet cream is dripping down her hand. Her mother is smiling beautifully; she's wearing a green dress and is barefoot. I know that person is her mother, because I know both of them.

That picture was taken by one of her father's friends; he had just bought the camera that weekend. He pulled up in front of their house excitedly and almost left his car keys in the ignition of his Toyota Cressida because he couldn't wait to show off his new toy. The little girl's mother was working in the garden; she never wears shoes when she's gardening. After the little girl had interrupted her mother with a million questions, the mother reached into the front pocket of her dress and pulled out a few coins: 'Marubini, please go and get an ice cream *ko* Jane.'

It was such a hot day and my ice cream was melting, but Baba insisted on me and Ma posing for the picture. I only held that picture in my hands once and then it was locked up in Ma's precious photo album. I wasn't allowed to page through the album by myself, an adult always had to hold it for me. 'These are our memories, Marubini, I want to make sure they stay safe.'

I look at the rest of the sketches and the man in all of them resembles my father. If Baba had lived and spent a long time out in the sun, he would look like that man. The man's skin looks dark and leathery. The bottoms of his feet are heavily calloused and he is perpetually hunched over. I study the sketches more closely and in the man's face I see both Simphiwe and myself. His posture is as if the sun and the earth have been trying to compress him, but there is a smile in his eyes. This man's eyes look at me so peacefully and beautifully that tears rush into my own eyes. I put my hand over his face. I can't bear to look at the sketches anymore.

'Rubi, could he be alive?'

'No, Sim.' The words that come out of my mouth hurt me. 'Baba is dead.'

Simphiwe collects his papers and puts them into his backpack. He doesn't say anything, but I sense that he still doesn't believe me. I wipe my face and take a sip of wine. The mere possibility of Baba being alive, while knowing that he couldn't possibly be, makes me nauseous with sadness.

Simphiwe still hasn't finished with the topic. 'All Ma identified was a charred body. You only have the word of a neighbour who didn't actually see them set him alight.' The word 'alight' escapes delicately out of his mouth. It's still a new idea for him and the possibility of his father's life ending in flames stings him.

'Simphiwe, the man had red little shoes burned into his hands.'

'So what, Rubi?' He is getting angry. 'What if that person stole the shoes from Baba on the train?'

I am not angry; just separate. A part of me is standing next to me, watching Simphiwe and I with interest. The other part is trying to make sense of the conversation.

'If he's alive, then why didn't he come back home, Sim?' My voice is trembling as I say it. I'm feeling breathless. I try to stand up and my feet collapse beneath me. No, this is not happening again! The room is blurring around me. I feel Simphiwe's hand on mine and the room steadies a little.

'Just sit for a while, Ru.' He pushes the glass of wine away from me protectively and hands me a glass of water. Words are falling out of my mouth with no real shape or form. I know I'm not making sense, but I want to tell Simphiwe that our father would never abandon us. As soon as Simphiwe lifts his hand off mine to call the waitress over, the room starts spinning again. I can't make it stop. It's too fast and I want to get off.

'Rubi?' I want to answer but the darkness gets to me before I can.

'It's the heat.' Simphiwe's hand is on my shoulder and his voice is floating above my head.

'Yeah, a lady actually fainted outside yesterday.' The waitress's face hovers over me. She smiles and asks if I'm okay. I nod and Simphiwe's face appears next to the waitress's.

'Are you okay to stand up?' I nod again.

The bill is settled and then we are walking towards Ma's car.

On both sides of the car is the distinctive green branding of her florist company: Jabulani Flowers. The logo is made up of vines that curve into the words that make up the company name. It's weird to think that Ma now has two nurseries in Soweto and a bigger one in Orange Grove. She was so happy when she got the contract to provide flowers for her former employer's company. With her own hardworking hands and her natural talent with flowers, she has built up her small florist business into a thriving livelihood.

When we reach the car Simphiwe seems nervous at the prospect of driving.

'Driving in Jozi is different from driving in Cape Town,' he says.

'Really, Sim? You're always complaining about not driving and now you are scared to take the wheel?'

He laughs. 'I'm not scared. I just think maybe we should sit here for a while.'

'Until *neng*?' I ask. I open up the take-away box from the restaurant and start eating my burger.

Simphiwe laughs. 'You were fainting a few minutes ago and now you're eating.'

'*Ja*, but what must I do if I'm hungry? Maybe that's why *ke fainta*.'

His lips are smiling but his eyes are not. 'Is it really crazy to think that my father is alive and that he is somehow reaching out to me through my sketches?'

I open my mouth to say, 'Yes, it's crazy' but then I see his face. My little brother looks so sad. I realise he is just trying to make sense of his gift. Gogo's comment was, 'We will have to watch and see how it develops.' Nkgono doesn't seem to think it's permanent either. 'Sometimes people do extraordinary things when the moment requires strength,' was her opinion.

Ma didn't say anything about Simphiwe's sketches. But whenever he was busy with them, working away quietly like a man possessed, she would sit at a safe distance just watching, like a lioness waiting to pounce on any predator that might surprise her cubs.

'No, it's not crazy, Sim. Many things seem crazy until they're proven not to be, right?'

He nods and starts the car.

Having eaten my fill of Christmas food, family members and neighbours dropping by, endless questions about Cape Town, marriage and having to sit listening to updates about people who I vaguely know, I slip out to go and sit in the nursery. It's cool and quiet in here and at least I can gather my thoughts. Sometimes it feels like I'm in a dream. We'll be sitting in the house happily talking and then Ma's voice will start to sound distant and Gogo will fade out like a mirage and before I know it I am stuck in a nightmare in my head.

I've begun to feel a certain sense of dread before bedtime. I don't want to deal with the little girl who keeps waking me up at night. She makes me relive the worst two days of my life. She drags me forward by the hand to make sure we both remember the same things. 'And remember how he stuck his tongue in your mouth while you were lying on the floor coughing up water and passing out?' She points to the wet floor in the man's room. I can't bear to think of his name or his face.

The screaming wakes me up and the nausea keeps me awake.

When sleep creeps in quietly and tries to lie down next to me, the little girl screams 'No!'

Nkgono says it's the natural way of things. 'I would be amazed if after all you went through you just got up, dusted yourself down and went back to Cape Town.' When Ma is not at her office then she is hovering around both Simphiwe and I. She doesn't say many words about what's happening to us. It's as if she doesn't know what to say. But she listens. She listens for my cries at night, the way I sigh when reliving the nightmares; and she listens for the sounds the pencil makes on paper when Simphiwe sketches pictures sent to him through dreams.

Gogo's patience is what unnerves me most. She doesn't want to say what any of this means. 'How can I diagnose something I have not observed? Who is to say whether it's trauma or the Calling? We just need to stand still and the answers will come.' If she detects a hint of discomfort in me, she will give me herbs or a pinch of some ground-up substance that she sources from her collection of healer's secrets. 'Don't ask me what it is. Do you not trust me? Stop asking me things I can't tell you.' She always says that with a smile and a wink. 'How else am I supposed to have my secrets? People come to me because I possess very strong secrets.'

I grew up around the smell of working soil; soil that is fertile, pregnant and always going through some magical process. The nursery has become my safe place. The earthy smells soothe my weary mind. Footsteps approach and I know that this peace will soon be gone too.

Ma walks in and scans my face. 'Are you okay?' I nod and she sits down on the wall next to me. 'You know, I wish I had the answers, Marubini. I wish I could fix all of this ...' She sighs and gazes at her flowers. We listen to each other breathe and I put my head on her shoulder.

'I don't expect you to fix anything, Ma. Gogo says we have to be patient and just wait it out.'

She laughs. 'Yhu, I'm only patient with plants. With them, there's a limited number of outcomes. I always know what my plants will do. And when something goes wrong, most times it's because I have done something wrong.' My mother smells like soil and freshly cut grass. She always has. I inhale her and close my eyes. She starts talking and her voice sounds like it's walking away from me.

'You know, Jabu and I always wanted to be parents. He wanted a family and I wanted to give him that. When I fell pregnant the first time, we were both so happy. Jabu would wake up and sing songs to my belly ... Then I lost that baby. I was sad, but hopeful that in time we would be parents.'

I open my eyes to look at her. She's sinking her fingers into the soil and playing with it in her hands as she speaks. 'You lose seven bellies and you give up hope. Jabu kept telling me it would be okay. We could still be happy together. Just the two of us. My friends always told me how lucky I was to have such an understanding mother-in-law. Mam'Thoko didn't do any of the things that mothers-in-law do. Some women have to contend with being called ugly names because they cannot have children. A mother-in-law will even sometimes encourage her son to have children outside the marriage. Mam'Thoko wasn't like that. She offered to find out if our trouble was something that had to do with ancestors. I refused and she understood. Both her and Jabu remained hopeful.

'When I fell pregnant with you, I was in agony. I didn't want to lose you, but I also didn't want to get my hopes up. Your father said to me, "This is the one, Kosha, I can feel it." I didn't believe him; I was afraid to love you.'

She squeezes sand into her palm then opens her hand to release it. 'When you didn't come when you were supposed to, I thought for sure you were dead inside me. You were so big that you weren't moving as much as you used to. At night I would poke at you and drink cold water just to feel you move. The day I finally saw you, it rained and I felt like you were telling me that it's okay to be happy again. It's okay to be hopeful. Out of all of my babies, you were the one who made it.' She smiles at me and dusts the dirt off her hands. 'Mama was right, you came out dark and polished like a queen from an ancient civilisation. I couldn't believe my eyes. You were alive and breathing. All that heartache and doubt was gone. You were worth the months of nausea and the sleepless nights ...' Ma stops speaking and her eyes grow wide. Her hands slide down the front of her dress quickly and she wipes them on the perfectly clean dress. Then my mother throws her head back and laughs. She laughs until tears roll down her face. I'm very confused.

'*Ma, ke eng?*'

She just keeps on laughing, hand to her stomach, shaking her head and crying from laughing so hard.

Nkgono walks, smiling, into the nursery, ready to join the laughter. 'What's so funny?'

I shrug. Nkgono and I look at my mother. Her face is still stuck in laughter but she is trying to compose herself. She really wants to explain but laughter is winning the tug of war.

Nkgono sits down next to me and we wait for Ma to stop laughing. It occurs to me that I haven't seen her laugh like this in years. My mother has been so wrapped up in this big, dark secret she was carrying that she was living a laboured life. There is music in this laughter of hers. She is laughing a painful melody of freedom. Freedom that she never thought would be hers because, being my mother, she would have taken our secrets to the grave with her. Her laughter slows down finally and then falls back into her chest.

'I can't believe three women like us couldn't figure it out,' she says, smiling broadly.

Nkgono leans on her stick and lifts herself off the wall. 'Figure what out?'

'She is pregnant.' My mother is pointing at me. I look down to where she's pointing, but nothing looks different. Nkgono also begins to laugh. Her laughter is big and sounds like thunder. The thunder tickles me a little; my cheeks grow warm and I smile.

'Why are you saying that I'm pregnant? You don't know that, Ma.'

Nkgono pokes at me, and now it is she who starts laughing. 'Oh *ja*, look at how big your bum is.'

I immediately turn my head to look at my behind. This makes them laugh even more. Realising what Nkgono just did, I give in and join the laughter. The laughter reaches into my bones and pulls out the black sticky stuff that has been plaguing me at night.

I laugh until I'm dizzy and need to sit down.

'*Ja*, she truly is pregnant,' Nkgono muses.

Thanks to the laughter, I am able to fall asleep easily that night. I'm not convinced that I am pregnant. But proving my mother and grandmother wrong is a mission for someone who has slept. Baba calls to me in my dreams. His voice is soft and gentle. He just keeps saying my name until I wake up and he is right there, sitting at the foot of my bed. He looks old but not frail. His hair is dusted with grey. I crawl out of bed and put my arms around him. His skin feels like leather and he is burned almost as dark as me. All he has on is a red cloth around his waist, and the smell of his old hut fills my room. I can't stop looking at my father; it's as if he walked straight off one of the sketches Simphiwe showed me earlier that week.

'Baba, you're alive ...'

'Nobody ever really dies.' His voice sounds much younger than he looks.

'But Ma went to go and identify your body when ...'

He shakes his head and smiles at me.

'I made a hasty decision. I didn't know how I was going to explain that I had to go away and carry our pain to the ancestors.'

I sit as close to him as I can, drinking in the sight of him. He stops talking and stares into my eyes. There are orange sparks in his brown eyes. I get closer and I see that there is movement inside Baba's eyes. It looks like many people walking around a place. I recognise this place: it's Small Street in Johannesburg city centre; the day of my birthday. I know this because I will never forget the last clothes I saw my father dressed in: brown pants that he hardly ever wore and a black shirt that Ma had spent a long time ironing. They argued about him choosing a shirt with creases on a morning when Ma had no time to iron it for him. He is standing inside a shop, paying for shoes and making conversation with the woman behind the till. She is not really into the conversation, but Baba is in a good mood and keeps talking. He makes his way to OK Bazaars and heads straight for the bakery section. There is a cake with granadilla pulp on top. He likes the look of that one.

'*Ngicela lena, sisi,*' he says to the woman behind the counter.

'*Ikhekhe* during the week? What's the occasion?'

Baba smiles. '*Indodakazi yami* is celebrating her birthday.'

The woman behind the counter hands him the cake. 'What a lucky girl. *Uhambe kahle, baba.*'

From the cake shop Baba heads to Park Station. It's a long walk but the time seems to fly. The train is fairly empty, so he puts the two plastic bags on the seat next to him. A few people he knows come onto the train and they discuss how things in the country might change. They discuss this quietly, though – you never know who may be listening these days, ready to report you to the overzealous members of one or another political party.

The conversation dries up and his acquaintances move on and leave him sitting by himself. Baba starts humming absent-mindedly to himself. He ignores the group of young guys who have come onto the train. They are watching him suspiciously.

'Hey, Inkatha!' one of the guys shouts to my father, implying that he is a supporter of the IFP.

Baba doesn't respond. The other people on the train pretend not to see or hear anything.

'Who are you supporting? You Zulus are ignorant killers!' another guy shouts. He is wearing a beret and seems to think himself the leader of the five young men.

Baba doesn't answer them. The beret guy has a scar down the side of his face; other than that he is a very handsome guy.

'We go away to become guerrillas and then you Zulus think you can just hijack the victory?' The beret guy is standing over my father and his face is being pulled to the side by anger.

Baba looks up at him and says, 'How did you know that I am *umZulu?*'

The young guy says, 'That stupid thing on your wrist.'

Baba never takes his eyes off the angry young man with the scar. 'Oh, *is'phandla*. Yes, I am *umZulu* and I am also *isangoma*.' He indicates the beads on his ankles as he says this.

A stocky young guy with a knife concealed under his shirt approaches Baba and the scarred guy. He seems to have a nervous disposition and keeps stroking the knife under his shirt reassuringly.

'Why are you talking to this guy? Let's get him off this train and finish him.' Stocky says this to Scar under his breath. Scar gives his nervous friend a dirty look.

'Are you crazy, *wena*? This man is a healer. He's not like those crazy Zulus who are killing our comrades. Get away from here!'

He pushes his friend away and turns his attention back to Baba. He claps his hands together twice as a sign of respect. '*Thokoza, Gogo,*' he says. While Scar explains to my father that his grandmother was also *isangoma*, Stocky and the rest of the crew have found themselves another 'umZulu'. This time it's a man wearing an IFP shirt. He is shouting back at them. The other passengers are getting nervous. The train stops and a chase ensues. Bodies are disembarking as others get on.

Baba gets up quickly, grabs his two plastic bags and follows the youths who are chasing their new target. He seems unsure of what he's doing, but he keeps chasing after them anyway. They run into a neighbourhood of shacks and Baba slows down for a minute.

'What are you doing, Jabulani?' I hear his thoughts. 'Those kids will kill you too.' He rests his arm against the wall and places the plastic bags on the floor. Screams come from a few roads away and Baba holds his breath. A little boy walks out of the shack and looks at Baba curiously. His mother runs after him and starts scolding him for running out of the house naked. The boy smiles at Baba.

'Take that child inside, there are some bad men running around here,' Baba says urgently. Grateful and scared, she nods and takes her child inside, locking the door behind her.

More screams reach Baba's ears. He sees the young men running back in the direction that they came from – young, agile bodies running from a horrible scene. A few people appear at their windows and then close them quickly. Nobody wants to be a witness to the violence, lest they be questioned by the police. No good will come from that. The police might torture them and accuse them of being terrorists who were involved in the attack. And should they survive that, some overzealous political party supporter might try to necklace them for being a police informer. People had even stopped trusting their own neighbours, because somehow the police had a way of knowing who to target.

Baba follows the smell of burning flesh and petrol until he finds the Inkatha-shirt man burning and screaming. He throws the plastic bags down in horror. He knows it's too late to do anything for the burning man. The mind works fast in such situations, and his mind orders him to throw the shoes into the fire of petrol and melting skin. The burning man grabs at what is being thrown at him. He's not screaming anymore. His mouth is open, but no sounds come out; the fire is eating way at his throat and his lungs.

'It's now or never,' a voice says to my father. He turns away from the dying man with the Judy Garland ruby slippers burning into his hands. 'There is no turning back now; better to be thought dead than to have abandoned them. They would never understand.'

The sparks in my father's eyes are the flames engulfing the man we buried.

'Why, Baba?'

'I had to. I was carrying that black blood of yours with me everywhere I went. I was too afraid to leave it here. It was weighing all of us down. I carried it in a bag with me day after day, under my shirt. I was the guardian of your pain, Marubini.'

'Where did you go when you left us?' He doesn't answer me. Just lifts his arms and puts them round me. I cry against him silently. 'Will I ever see you again?' More silence. He lets me cry more tears then lifts my face up. 'I can never come back. My burden has been removed, but I have been instructed by the ancestors never to return.'

'Where are you?'

A small smile but no answer. 'I walked for years with this burden weighing down on me. When I reached my destination, I was relieved of it and you were freed too ...'

'No! No, no, no, no ... please come back.'

He raises his hand to signal that he wants me to stop talking. 'That's not up to me. I want you to know that you are not stuck. You are free now.'

He kisses my forehead and gets up from the bed. He is not as tall as I remember him. He stands slightly hunched over. 'UBaba uyak'thanda, Marubini.' After he tells me that he loves me, my father becomes a snake. A beautiful white and red snake that slithers away and turns into water. The water evaporates and leaves my room smelling like burning herbs; the smell of my father the water snake.

I climb back into bed and cry myself to sleep.

'Ru. Wake up, Ru. *Vuka!*'

I open my eyes to see a younger version of my father standing where the old, hunched-over version was standing.

'I think you're having a bad dream,' Simphiwe says. He sits down on the bed next to me. Then he says, 'I think I know where Baba is.'

'Cameroon?' Nkgono says. 'Why do you want to know about Cameroon?'

Simphiwe is getting impatient on the back seat. 'Nkgono, is it possible or not?'

My grandmother shoots Simphiwe an angry glare and he sits back, defeated.

We're driving Nkgono back to her house. This visit is the longest she has stayed in Soweto. 'I can't just pack up and leave my place forever, Makosha. I left my house in the charge of my cousin's child. Who knows what that silly girl is doing to my animals and garden?'

Ma was not very happy when Nkgono told her that she was going home. The flower business was busy so she asked Simphiwe and me to take our grandmother back to Pietersburg.

All Nkgono wanted to talk about was the baby.

'*Eeeh, leJeremane la hao …*'

Simphiwe laughs and corrects her. 'Pierre is French, Nkgono, not German.'

Nkgono gives Simphiwe another stare that makes him focus on the trees that are running by his window.

'*Ja*, this French guy … You say he is happy about the baby. And he wants to marry you?'

I laugh and shake my head. 'Nkgono, I don't know if Pierre wants to get married, but I'm happy just the way we are.' Ever since Pierre found out about the pregnancy, he has been calling every day to check how the baby is. I keep telling him that nothing has changed between calls and it's still baking in the oven. 'Would you open the oven door every five minutes while you're baking to check how it's coming on?' I ask him. 'No! Then stop asking me about your baby every five minutes.'

The silence in the car disturbs Simphiwe. He leans forward to switch on the radio. Nkgono slaps his hands from the controls.

'Do you want to hear about Cameroon or not?' She has his attention. '*Rona, batho* are not from here. We've been here so long and stopped telling our stories so far back that we have forgotten our real home. This place that you call Cameroon is more or less where we come from. That is how it happened with us Bantu. Any family will tell you that even when you love each other very much, you cannot live together forever. So we split up and moved away from our old home. This movement of Batho or Bantu, whichever you prefer, was one of the biggest movements of a single group of people in Africa. Not even the chosen people of this God that the missionaries brought here migrated in such large numbers. You see your sister Marubini? You see how dark and shiny and beautiful she is? That's what we all used to look like. But as we moved further and further away from the sun and from our source, we changed. Not only did our skin colour change, but we could no longer understand each other properly. Those white men came here and changed us further. They told us that we were different from each other and that all the practices that kept us connected were barbaric.' Nkgono's voice is both soothing and coarse.

Simphiwe sits back and listens without interrupting Nkgono. She is lamenting the loss of our identity and history. 'In the schools they teach children history according to when white men arrived here. Then we walk around believing that we did not exist intelligently and peacefully before that stupid man from the spice company came.' This makes me giggle.

When we get to Nkgono's house Simphiwe jumps out the car and carries her bags inside. We don't stay long because we have to drive back to Johannesburg.

'When are you going to come and see me again, Marubini? You know you used to live here. This is still your home.'

I hug Nkgono tightly and say, 'I know that, Koko.' She slaps my arm playfully. 'It's too late for that, you township child.'

Simphiwe and Nkgono hug and then we get back into the car. It feels wrong to be leaving so soon, but Pierre arrives in Johannesburg tonight. I miss him. I feel like we have so much to talk about. All I want is to feel his arms around me while I listen to him talk about food and annoying customers. In the seat next to me Simphiwe is sighing and looking at one of his sketches. It's a puddle of water with what looks like a footprint in the middle. He thinks that this puddle is a sign of where Baba is.

'That could be anywhere, Sim.'

He shakes his head. 'This puddle is clearly in the shape of Cameroon, Ru. It's exactly the shape of that country and you know it.'

I sigh and nod. He's right; the puddle is in the shape of Cameroon. Simphiwe drew it a few nights before I had my dream about Baba – before Sim had any idea of the Cameroon connection. He is the only person I've told about the dream. He stayed up late on many nights trying to figure out what the puddle represented.

We went through a few possibilites until Simphiwe came up with the bright idea of comparing its shape to maps of countries. 'We're gonna start in Africa because ... duh ...!'

'You're getting really good at working out what your sketches mean. I'm proud of you, Sim.'

He smiles and carries on trying to decipher the puddle that he sketched. I have no idea whether he's right about the Cameroon connection, or whether we would find Baba still alive in Cameroon or not. All I know is that Simphiwe needs me to believe him. I remember how lost I felt when nobody believed that I was not trying to kill myself. I am choosing to believe my little brother. No matter where his puddle may lead us.

The road back to Johannesburg is one that I could drive with my eyes closed. Ma and I have driven this road so many times together. Nkgono has also made this trip many times: to see where her daughter had chosen to live; to attend a wedding; to answer the summons to come and deliver a stubborn baby who didn't want to arrive; and again, to return a wounded grandchild who was thrust into her arms after she herself lost her husband.

It was our last night together. The other girls were all much older than me. Nkgono pulled me aside and told me how proud she was of me. 'You learned a lot of difficult things and you may not really be a woman in the eyes of the world but you are more educated about being a woman than most women in the world.' She kissed me on the forehead and sent me to go and get ochre smeared on my body.

When Nkgono told me about *lebollo* and that I would have to go too, I was scared. 'Don't be scared. That is my job and I will make sure nobody hurts you.' The issue of *lebollo* was a highly contested one in Nkgono's village. She was the midwife and also the person in charge of ushering young girls into womanhood. Not all parents were keen on the idea of their young daughters taking this rite of passage.

'It is how the times are,' I heard Nkgono tell one of the women who helped her. 'People don't see the use for something that makes women stronger. They would encourage it if we were making sure that these girls *didn't* know how to be powerful and belong to themselves.' The first night, when we arrived at the camp that was a little way beyond the village, Nkgono made a very long speech. The older women in the gathering made 'mmmm' sounds and clapped throughout her speech.

'Most of you are here because you have started flowing like the ocean does with the moon. Others are here because, well, soon you will be considered too old.' She laughed a little as she said this. 'You will have been told by misinformed people that this is where you will learn to be good wives and how to pleasure your husbands.' Some of the older girls giggled. 'They are wrong, and you will be disappointed to find that men are hardly ever mentioned here.' It was the turn of the old women to laugh. 'We let people believe this error because otherwise we would not be allowed to teach you what we do. So now you can never tell anyone what you learn here ... ever. The people who will know are people who have been through this too. You are now part of an elite group of women who have been through this rite of passage and belong to themselves.'

In the days that followed we were divided into groups and taught many wonderful and shocking things by the old women who were in charge of this rite of passage. I got to know my mind, spirit and body better. We learned how to stay connected to our source and how we were connected to the forces of nature. Some of it was too much for me to take in. When Nkgono felt like I was in over my head she would talk to me at night when the other initiates were sleeping. While roasting peanuts over the fire she would break down the concepts into child-size pieces for me to understand.

With our freshly cut hair, bodies and faces smeared in ochre, we were almost ready to be presented back into the village. The sun was coming up to greet us as we sang songs that the old women had taught us.

'Nkgono, why am I the smallest girl here?'

Nkgono stopped singing and handed me my brown suitcase filled with my new clothes that I would wear now that I had been through this process.

'It's because you need to be here. You were sent to me to be guided through an important and necessary process. I want to make sure that your body and mind are speaking the same language.'

I took the bag and looked at her. 'Will you always guide me, even when I'm big?' She nodded, smiling, and took me to join the other girls. The old women were singing the loudest.

Nkgono stood in the front and inspected us; then she turned to the old women and shouted, 'Here are the women who return back home as their own wives!' They cheered in response and led the way as we walked back to the village that we had left two weeks before. Everybody in the entire village was awake and they started cheering as we arrived. The morning cold was making me shiver. The older girls were topless, too, but they were not shivering.

Nkgono looked so proud of me that I pretended I was not cold. We stood in a straight line in front of the whole village – a long snake made up of ochre, bare-breasted, bald-headed female bodies standing proudly. The village women who had been through the process sang along with us. They were the happiest out of everyone. They waved and winked at us. My mother was in the crowd, singing and crying. I stood up taller and sang louder at the sight of her. She never took her eyes off me.

I felt very important on that day. All the homes that had an initiate slaughtered an animal and cooked a lot of food. Nkgono even slaughtered a goat for me. Long after visitors had come to congratulate my family on the achievement of their daughter and gone again, we sat on around the fire. My rogue goat was sleeping nearby. Nkgono was not in the least concerned that the goat was not locked up already. Ma and Nkgono washed the ochre off me in a zinc tub by the fire. I was happy to get the ochre off my skin; it had started drying and peeling off my face and it made the rest of my body feel tight. I had already asked more than ten times when I would be allowed to wash. Once I was clean again and smeared with goat fat to soften my skin, we sat quietly together. Ma was humming the songs that only an elite group of women would recognise.

'You are one of us now, Marubini,' Ma said sadly. Both she and Nkgono cried. Ma looked sad but Nkgono looked happy. I was just exhausted from the past few days and only wanted to sleep. That night I slept outside, between my mother and grandmother.

AMEN

Chari is reaching and kicking happily on my lap. Her fingers grab her chubby little foot and it heads into her mouth. Pierre walks in and picks her up. 'Your drinks are ready.'

I get up and Chari's empty bottle falls on the floor. Pierre looks at me and shakes his head: 'You won't stop till you've destroyed all of them.' I kiss him and place the empty bottle in his free hand. I head to the door where Unathi and Lian are exchanging pleasantries on the doorstep. 'Right this way, ladies, you are right on time for gin o'clock.'

We walk out onto the patio where the sun is shining beautifully.

'Where's Chari?' Unathi asks.

'Daddy is putting her down for her nap, otherwise we'll get no peace.'

I pour drinks and we sit by the poolside. I let my legs slip into the pool. The water fills the spaces between the red and white beads around my ankles.

'Chari is such a beautiful name, Maru, what does it mean?' Lian asks, cleaning her sunglasses with the edge of her shirt.

I smile and close my eyes. 'It's the name of a river in Cameroon, where I met my teacher.'

ACKNOWLEDGEMENTS

Pa for reading *The Yearning* when it was still a baby and correcting my 'Soweto Spelling'. Zakes Mda (mentor and BFF), for telling me my stories are worth telling. Vuyo Sokupa (my first writing partner). My editor, Elana Bregin, and publisher, Andrea Nattrass, for handling the weekly meltdowns and doubts. Nomali Minenhle Cele (my current writing partner). My family and friends who had no clue I was doing this but support all of my dreams. Everybody at Pan Macmillan who has made this possible. Marcee, *The Yearning* wouldn't exist if you weren't in my life ... neither would I.